Burning Brighter

Fireside Romance Book 2

Burning Brighter

Fireside Romance Book 2

by Drew Hunt

Fireside Romance Book 2: Burning Brighter

JMS Books LLC
10286 Staples Mill Rd. #221
Glen Allen, VA 23060
www.jms-books.com

Printed in the United States of America

ISBN: 9781466301887

For all those who read First Flames and asked for more, here's Burning Brighter. I hope you enjoy the continuing romantic journey of Simon and Mark.

Chapter 1

"THERE'S THAT FALLEN tree we sat on last time," I said. "Do you want to rest for a while?"

Mark and I were walking through the woods on Boxing Day.

He smiled. "I guess I should call it my confession log."

"If you want to sit somewhere else…."

"No, no, it's okay," Mark said, resting his head on my shoulder. "Last night was wonderful for me. It was like my first time all over again."

I grew embarrassed and found myself apologising. "You must think I'm…stupid for not being able to go all the way. I just—"

"Stop it." Mark gave me a squeeze. "Our friendship grew over time, so it seems only right our love life should do the same. And besides, I don't have any condoms."

Mark had refused to put me at risk. Although he'd undergone some blood tests in hospital, which had come back negative, he still worried that something from his former clients might still lie dormant inside him. Despite this, the previous night had been much more than I could have ever hoped for. The loving, the tenderness, the tears. Throughout, Mark had been gentle, kind, and supportive. Never in my wildest fantasies could I have believed being with another man could be so wonderful.

Mark started to shiver.

I kissed his neck. "Want to walk again?"

He leaned up and kissed me. "Please."

We got up and I dusted him down. It being fairly thickly wooded and with no one else about, we put our arms around each other.

"Do you think the nurse will keep your bandages off next time?"

"I don't know. My hands keep itching. She said that was a good sign. If I tell her that I'll be careful, maybe she won't wrap them. It'll be great to be able to use them again."

"It must be frustrating. The ward sister told me you might get upset because you couldn't do things for yourself, but I don't remember you getting that way."

"I've felt like I was going in that direction a time or two, but you've been absolutely great. You should have gone into nursing."

I shook my head. "I couldn't. I think the main reason why I'm able to help you is because I love you." I got a thrill saying that; I'd never said it to another person, apart from family members of course.

Mark—who had been forced to work the streets due to his dad kicking him out of the house—had suffered chemical burns to his hands when there'd been an explosion at his pimp's house. Jake—the pimp—had died, releasing Mark from the financial hold he'd been under. After I'd learned about Mark's accident, I'd rushed to his bedside and persuaded him to come and live with me. One thing had led to another and on Christmas morning we'd declared our love for each other.

Wow, I thought, *it's only been twenty-four hours. I can't believe it.*

"Did you always want to work in a library?" Mark asked, snapping me back to the present.

I nodded, embarrassed.

"What?"

"Remember, I'm a pretty repressed kind of guy. I didn't play outside much when I was little. When I was naughty, Mum would make me go outside as punishment, rather than send me to my room."

Mark chuckled.

"I've always liked the smell and the…I don't know, the potential for learning of a room full of books. That's why I studied library science at university."

"You went to uni?" he asked.

I nodded. "It was okay, I didn't join in the social activities as much as I should have though." Feeling the depressive thoughts—that were never far away—crowd in, I continued, "Look, Mark, I'm a boring, stay-at-home person. I hope I don't stifle you with all that."

"Stop it," Mark repeated. "Remember, I've known you for a few months now. And I've come to love that person very much."

"Thanks," I said softly, giving Mark a squeeze.

We walked a little further before he said, "The main reason why I left our house so often was to get away from Dad. I had a few friends in Newcastle, but no one really close, you know?"

"I know. I had one close friend, Patrick. I even thought at one point that I might have had a crush on him."

"What happened?"

"We were watching the telly one night, and something about the Stonewall Riots in New York came on. Patrick came out with some pretty horrible things about gay people. I was grateful for that programme. I slowly edged myself away from him after that. Saved me some heartache down the line I suppose. Anyway, his family moved down south and I haven't heard from him since."

"No great loss," Mark said, giving me a hug.

"No." I let out a breath.

"Want to head home?" Mark asked when we came to the edge of the woods.

"Might as well. I could do with a cup of coffee."

"Me, too," Mark said.

On the way home, I asked, "So, now you know all about my boring early life, what about your past?"

"You already know the basics; you wrote them on the unemployment benefit forms. I left school at sixteen with a small handful of O levels, nothing to get excited about. I worked in a café for a while, then got a job at a supermarket, stacking shelves, that kind of thing. It wasn't that interesting or well-paid—but I was glad to have a job. So many of my school friends just went straight on the dole."

"You were lucky. So was I. I couldn't believe it when I got the job at our local library. I thought I'd have to move. Hopefully one day I'll get a promotion. I've got the qualifications and now the work experience. Just waiting for the right opening I guess."

"Would you move?" Mark asked.

"I'd have to think about it, but I'd rather not. I'm settled where I am. I make enough to get by on, but it'd be nice to have a bit more to spend, and now I've got someone to spend it on…"

"So long as I can spend money on you, too, when I get some," Mark put in.

"Maybe I'll let you," I said with a chuckle. "The one thing I would do though, if I had the money, would be to buy a car."

"Have you passed your test?"

"Mum and Dad gave me a course of driving lessons as a present for passing my A levels. I thought about getting a car then, but everything was within walking distance at the university, and once I'd graduated I had enough debts without adding the costs of running a car."

Mark nodded.

"I'd take a refresher course before I got back behind the wheel. I don't have much practical experience of driving."

"I never learnt," Mark said. "When mum died, dad spent all his money on booze, and I didn't earn enough for lessons, much less for a car, insurance and the like."

"Well, once you've got yourself settled in a job, you might want to think about learning."

"We'll see."

We ambled back to the house in silence, each with our own thoughts. Once inside I took off our coats and asked Mark if he wanted a coffee and something to eat.

"Have we got any of that boiled ham left?"

"Yeah," I said after looking in the fridge. "A round of sandwiches will finish it off."

We'd just finished eating when there was a knock at the front door. I went to answer it.

It was Paul Bates and his fourteen-year-old son, Sam.

"Sorry to bother you," Paul said in a rush, "but Helen's waters have broken, and—"

"She's early," I said, then realised Paul didn't have time to debate such things. "Sorry. How can we help?"

"Would you mind looking after Sam? My parents are on holiday and—"

"No problem," I interrupted.

"Thanks." Paul dashed back down the street, leaving Sam standing on the doorstep, not looking terribly happy.

I gave Sam an encouraging smile, then stuck my head out of the door and called, "Paul! If you need to stay with Helen overnight, Sam can bunk on the sofa."

"Thanks." He waved before disappearing into his house.

Turning around, I saw that Mark had come into the living room. "This is Mark…a friend of mine." I told Sam, beckoning him inside. "Are you excited about having a baby brother or sister?"

"No, not really," came the meek reply. Sam's eyes were hiding behind long lashes, which I suspected many girls would envy.

"Why's that?" Mark asked.

"He or she will probably cry all night."

"But it'll be nice to watch the baby as he or she grows up, starts crawling, walking and talking."

"Suppose," Sam said with little enthusiasm. "What happened to your hands?" he asked Mark.

"Someone I knew was playing around with chemicals, and things went wrong. I should be okay in a week or so though."

"That's good." Sam smiled; he seemed to be warming up to Mark.

"Would you like anything to eat?" I asked Sam.

"No thanks. We just ate when Mum decided she needed to go to hospital."

"What about watching some television, or maybe a video?" I asked, pointing at the shelves of tapes. I felt out of my depth, never having had to keep a teenager entertained before.

He shrugged and walked over to the shelves.

"So, Sam, what are you studying at school?" Mark asked.

He shrugged again. "Oh, you know, the usual boring stuff."

I sighed. This wasn't going to be easy.

"There must be something you've done that you've enjoyed." Mark wasn't giving up.

"We've just finished a project on 1930s Britain. The differences between those who had a job, and those who didn't."

"My grandfather went on the Jarrow March," Mark said.

"Really?" Sam turned from examining the rows of video tapes. "Did you know the march was fifty years ago this year?"

"Really?" I asked,

"Yeah, 1936," Sam said. "Did your granddad say much about the march?" he asked Mark.

"He said he felt betrayed."

"Is your grandfather still alive?" I asked.

Mark shook his head. "He died a couple of years ago."

"Sorry," Sam said.

The subject moved back to the Jarrow March and Mark told us more about how it had affected the area where he'd grown up. "…basically the government couldn't have cared less about conditions in the traditional industries."

I had no idea Mark was so political.

"Things were a lot better for the newer industries like car making and electronics," Sam said.

"But most of that was in the Midlands and the South," Mark pointed out.

"That's true," Sam nodded.

The room grew quiet. Then Sam, who had gone back to choosing a film, said, "Can I watch this one?" He'd pulled out an action movie I'd bought for Mark but we'd never gotten around to watching.

"Of course," I said. "Put it in the machine and come and sit on the sofa."

Sam sat in the chair looking at first Mark then me.

"Is there anything wrong?" I asked.

"Erm…I, are you…I mean do you mind me asking, is Mark your boyfriend?"

I looked at Mark. He gave a slight nod.

"Would it bother you if we were?"

"God, no. My uncle Steve is gay, he's cool!"

"Do you get to see him much?" Mark asked.

"No, he lives in the north of Scotland. He doesn't have a boyfriend though. How long have you and Simon known each other?"

"A few months, but we only became boyfriends yesterday."

"Really? Wow, that's great!"

"I think so, too," Mark said.

I smiled, touched that Mark would say such a thing. But thinking we should change the subject, I said, "Shall we watch this film?"

❖

AFTER REWINDING THE video cassette, putting it in its case and back on the shelf—in alphabetical order, resulting in much teasing from the other two—I got us something to eat.

Sam was amused at first with me having to feed Mark, but after a while offered to do it.

We chatted a while longer about various things, until the phone broke in on a discussion we were having about Sam's teachers. Most of them I knew, as I'd gone to the same school. Mark of course couldn't add much to the conversation, so in a way I was glad of the phone interrupting us.

It was Paul. He told me Helen was in labour, but the midwife didn't expect her to deliver for a while yet. He reconfirmed that it was okay for Sam to stay with us, and then asked to speak to his son, so Mark and I went into the kitchen to give Sam some privacy.

"Seems like a good kid," Mark said.

"Yeah, I was amazed he had the balls to ask about us though. He's always seemed pretty shy to me. He seems to have taken a shine to you…asking if he could feed you. I hope I'm not going to have to fight him for your affections," I laughed.

"You don't think he's got a crush on me do you?"

"I couldn't blame him if he has, you're a real stud." I squeezed Mark's crotch, making him jump.

Sam chose that moment to walk in on us. He reddened, and started to back out of the room. "Sorry, I just wanted to tell you that I was nipping off home to get my sleeping bag and some other stuff."

"It's okay, Sam," I said.

"Uh, yeah." His blush increased. "I'll be back in about ten minutes."

"Leave the door on the latch, so you can let yourself back in."

❖

THE THREE OF us spent an enjoyable evening watching telly and talking. Sam was a very intelligent young man. He'd visited the library a few times, and had borrowed books on a wide range of subjects.

Mark asked Sam what he wanted to do after leaving school.

"I suppose I'll go to university."

"What will you study?" I asked.

"Probably history. I don't really fancy ancient or medieval much. We did some stuff on the Romans a few years ago, but I like the more modern stuff better."

"What would you say was your favourite period?" Mark enquired.

"Erm, the Second World War I think. We went to the Imperial War Museum in London on a school trip once. That was great."

"Would you like to work in a museum?" I asked.

"Hadn't really thought that far ahead, but it's something to think about."

I'd visited some museums in York, and a few had really made an effort to engage the visitor. Very few things were stuck in glass cases. I'd found the whole experience to be quite fascinating.

The clock eventually showed it was bedtime. I asked Sam to go to the bathroom first, then Mark and I would use it. After we had all washed and changed into our night attire, we bid each other goodnight.

THE PHONE RANG at seven the next morning. Mark and I were still in bed, so I took the call on the bedroom extension. It was Paul. I went downstairs, and got Sam to the phone. Mark and I quickly washed and dressed, and went back downstairs. Sam announced he had a baby sister. She was small and in an incubator, but the doctors said she would be fine.

"I hope you got a good night's sleep," Mark said to Sam,

"because when she comes home, you might not get many more."

Sam groaned. "Can I come and sleep on your couch if that happens?"

I ruffled his hair and said, "We'll see." Somehow I didn't think Paul and Helen would agree to such an arrangement.

I got on with making our breakfast. Sam offered to help, and he insisted on feeding Mark. *Yes*, I thought, *I'll have to watch those two.*

During breakfast, I said, "Sorry, Sam, but in all the excitement I forgot to ask what your new sister's name will be."

"Charlotte Elizabeth."

"Aw. That's sweet," Mark said.

Sam frowned.

"I'm sure she'll be lovely once you get to know her."

"I've told Mum, there is no way I'm going to change a smelly nappy."

Mark and I laughed.

"You'll come around. You'll want to help your parents as much as possible I'm sure. A baby takes an awful lot of looking after. Your mum and dad will need all the help they can get," I said.

"We'll see," Sam said before taking another bite of toast.

Once we'd finished eating, Sam helped me clear away the breakfast things.

"Come on," I said, "We're going into town to get baby Charlotte a present to welcome her when she gets home."

Sam didn't seem overly enthusiastic at the prospect, but tagged along anyway.

We went into a few shops, but we couldn't agree on what to buy. Eventually we settled on a musical mobile to hang over the cot.

As we turned into our street, Sam spotted his dad's car outside their house. He went home to see what the latest news was.

Mark and I continued to our place. As both of us had been only children, we couldn't really identify with Sam's predicament. But we decided it would have been quite nice to have a younger sister. Mark said he wasn't sure if he'd have preferred a younger brother though. I had to agree. Females were such strange creatures.

THE REST OF the weekend passed uneventfully. Paul popped round to thank us for looking after Sam, and for the nursery mobile. He reported that Helen had had a painful labour. So much so, at one point she'd said rather loudly in front of the doctor and midwife, "You're having a vasectomy, you bastard."

Both Mark and I instinctively reached for our crotches. Paul laughed.

It seemed that Helen would spend a day or two in hospital. Hopefully they would be able to bring Charlotte home in about a week's time.

Chapter 2

MARK AND I went back to see the nurse about his bandages on Monday morning. She said that although things were healing nicely, Mark would have to keep his hands wrapped for another week.

"I'm sorry, love," Mark said.

The fact he was apologising to me, when he was the one who had suffered the greatest, made my heart swell up with love. I hugged him in front of the nurse. Normally I wasn't so demonstrative in public, but the moment called for it. The nurse gave us a strange look.

I turned to her and said, "Have you got a problem?"

I don't think she was expecting such a challenge, so backed down. Mark later told me he had been proud of me.

❖

THE REST OF the week flew by. Mark and I, celebrating the New Year, stood in front of the telly in each other's arms watching Big Ben strike midnight and then sang Auld Lang Syne. We'd been invited to a party given by Mary's parents, as well as to a smaller gathering hosted by Paul and Helen, but we both wanted to see in our first New Year alone together.

The following Monday, Mark's bandages finally came off. I could only begin to imagine what a relief it must be for him. The nurse, a different one this time, cautioned Mark to take things easy. She told him not to get his hands wet too often.

"Does that mean I can get out of the washing up?" he asked hopefully.

"No, you can still dry the pots." She had his number.

After cashing a prescription for some ointment for Mark, we decided to go to Daphne's for lunch.

"How do your hands feel?" Mary, who was in the café on her break, asked Mark.

"Bloody marvellous," he said, picking up his cup of hot chocolate.

"Excellent," Mary smiled. So you'll be able to do the washing up now."

I laughed and Mark rolled his eyes.

"What?" Mary looked confusedly between the two of us.

"Long story," I told her.

She shrugged. "So, Simon, you'll be coming back to work soon then?"

I hadn't thought about it. "I've got a couple of days leave still to go. I've also got another week's worth in reserve which I'll have to use up before April or I'll lose it."

"True," Mary said. "But I've missed you so much, darling." She fluttered her eyelashes at me.

"Daft bat!" I said.

We laughed.

"It's just not the same without you there."

"I want to spend as much time as I can with my man," I said quietly, taking Mark's free hand under the table.

It was fantastic to finally be able to hold his hand. Even though we had to be careful about it in public.

Mary saw what we were doing and gave us a wide smile.

MARK'S UNEMPLOYMENT BENEFIT money started coming through. He offered me some of it to put towards his keep. I refused to take a penny.

"Look, apart from a bit of extra food, it's really not much dearer to have two people living here."

When we got to the supermarket that Thursday afternoon, Mark wanted to pay. We didn't need much, as we still had a load of food in from the holidays. I told him he could pay for the Chinese take-away. This seemed to mollify him. I asked if he had already chosen what he wanted to order. I remembered what Mark had said about how when he'd been a child, on the way home from the supermarket his parents would stop off at a Chinese take-away, and so as they shopped he would have to decide what he wanted to eat

Mark laughed.

As we sat at the table eating our meal, I realised this simple domestic tableau was deeply symbolic of our lives now. Previously I could order only the one dish. With Mark here, we could each get a different dish and share. As a result the variety that the meal now gave us was a far richer experience because of that simple act of sharing. If we expanded this to the rest of our relationship, who knew what wonderful possibilities awaited us in the future?

ONE FRIDAY AT the end of January, I walked up the garden path, musing at what a long and boring day it had been at the library. I'd telephoned Mark at home earlier to tell him not to bother cooking, as we'd have a bar meal down at the Mucky Duck.

"Lucy, I'm home!" I said, closing the front door behind me.

Mark and I were both confirmed *I Love Lucy* fans.

"Good day at the office, dear?" Mark gave me a hug and a kiss to the cheek.

"The usual. Mary sends her best. Mind you, she's over the moon now Jerry's back."

"I bet, she really took it hard over Christmas."

Mary's boyfriend, Jerry, was a post-graduate history student who had gone on a field trip to the Middle East over Christmas.

"He's taking her out to the cinema tonight. Back row and all that. Then they're going out for a romantic candlelit meal at that new Italian that's just opened up on the high street," I said, taking off my coat.

"We'll have to go and try it out sometime," Mark said.

"Good idea. I'll ask Mary what she thought about it on Monday."

"She'll have been too busy gazing into Jerry's eyes to take any notice of the food."

"You're probably right," I chuckled.

"Anyway, what kind of a day have you had?"

"Same old, same old." Mark was not happy about being stuck at home all day with little to occupy him.

"Something will turn up soon, my angel."

"I know. It's just so frustrating. I don't like the idea of living off you."

I wrapped him in a tight hug. "There's millions out there in a similar position, but it won't be long before an employer sees what a wonderful and talented guy you are."

"Thanks. I don't know what I'd do without you."

"And I don't know what I'd do without you either." I pinched him on the cheeks.

Mark went upstairs and took a bath.

It was these small and, by themselves, insignificant domestic arrangements which enriched my life immeasurably. I remembered another example of this: we had been standing at the kitchen sink one evening after dinner. I must have zoned out, because the next thing I'd known Mark was speaking.

"You're going to wipe the pattern off that plate."

"Huh? Sorry, I was just thinking about how great all this is," I had said, waving the washing-up brush over the whole scene. "I mean, who'd have thought such a mundane activity as doing the washing up could be such, such…" I hadn't been able to find the words.

"Know what you mean. It's great just being with you. That's the best way I can put it, just being here with you."

I'd dropped the brush into the sink and put my arms around him.

I was jolted back to the present by Mark kissing me on top of the head and telling me the bathroom was free. Damn, I'd wanted to wash his back…or something.

I WAS SOAKING in the warm water when the phone rang. It didn't ring for long; Mark must have answered it.

Later, when I went into the bedroom, Mark was fastening the final button on his new blue shirt. "Your Gran was on the phone," he said, buttoning his cuffs.

Damn! I'd forgotten to ring her New Year's Day.

"She was wondering if we wanted to go see her next weekend."

Realising I'd gotten away with not calling, I quickly recovered. "Can't see why not, we've nothing arranged, have we?" I asked, pulling a clean pair of underpants from the drawer. There was one benefit of Mark being home all day, I always had clean underwear.

"Don't think so."

I ran through the bus timetables in my head. "Should take us a couple of hours, including changing buses in Leeds."

"I'll take a book to read or something to help pass the time."

"I'll probably do the same. I've really neglected my reading since you came along." I ran my hands along his broad shoulders. "But you've proved to be a really sexy distraction." I started to kiss him.

"Keep that up," Mark said when he drew back for breath, "and we'll never be ready to go out and eat."

"We haven't booked a table or anything, so it doesn't matter what time we turn up."

We spent several more minutes kissing. I also managed to undo most of the buttons on Mark's shirt before he smacked my underwear-clad bottom.

"That's from your Gran for not ringing her on New Year's Day."

WE ARRIVED AT the Mucky Duck at about 8 pm, an hour or so later than we had originally planned. After getting our drinks from the bar, we were in the process of looking for an empty table when Paul and Helen spied us.

"Simon, Mark." Paul stood. "Do you want to join us? It's a bit crowded, and you'd probably have to wait a while for a table."

"Thanks," Mark said. "It is a bit busy."

"Yeah, it seems like half the town has decided to spend the evening out," Helen put in.

"So, how are you both?" I asked Helen. We hadn't seen either of them in over a week.

"Good." Helen smiled. "Though we're glad we were able to get a babysitter for a couple of hours so we could get out."

I smiled. "And how's Charlotte?

"She's great," Paul said. "Filling nappies at an alarming rate.

A bit of financial advice for you. Buy shares in Pampers."

We all laughed.

"Last time we saw Sam he didn't seem all that thrilled about having a younger sister," I said. "Has he changed his mind?"

Both Paul and Helen's faces dropped.

"No. He still doesn't want anything to do with her," Helen said.

"I hoped he would have come around by now. But..." Paul took a drink of his lager.

"Sam said he was worried about getting a good night's sleep," Mark put in.

Paul set his glass back on the table. "Charlotte certainly does her fair share of crying."

"No more than most babies surely?" I questioned.

"No, the health visitor said there was nothing to worry about there," Helen said. "We just can't seem to get Sam involved with his sister at all. The health visitor suggested Sam should spend a few days with a friend or relative, but that's not practical what with school and everything."

"We'd love to have him come stay at our place, but we've only the one bedroom." I took a pull on my pint of bitter, feeling sympathy for the Bates' plight.

Although I'd never told Paul and Helen that Mark and I were boyfriends, they knew I was gay, and that I only had the one bedroom. So it didn't take a genius to work out we were sleeping together. However, as they accepted me as being gay, I knew they wouldn't have a problem with Mark and me. Also, as they allowed Sam to stay with us when Charlotte was born, it didn't seem they had a problem with him spending time with us. They must have known Sam often visited our house.

"When old Maurice Johnson owned the house, I had plans drawn up for him to have the loft converted into another bedroom, but he never could commit himself to me doing the work for him." Paul was a builder. He had overseen the building of the sound and video extension to the library. "If you two are interested in having me convert the loft I'd give you a competitive estimate. Especially if you have it done soon. Winter is always a slow time in the construction business. And with you two being so local and everything."

"Forgive my husband, he's always trying to drum up new business," Helen added. We all laughed.

"I'd love to see the plans, but at the moment money is a bit tight," I said.

"I'll bring the plans over in the next couple of days. No pressure."

"Thanks," Mark put in.

A second bedroom would be useful, especially if my parents or Gran wanted to stay over.

We spent an enjoyable evening at the pub, chatting and eating, and later the four of us walked back to our street together.

"I better go see if the babysitter has managed to keep the peace between the children," Helen said.

"It can't be that bad, surely," Mark said with concern.

"So long as Sam is left alone and doesn't have to have anything to do with Charlotte, he behaves." Paul sighed.

"If it'll help, we could have another word with him," I said.

"It couldn't do any harm." Helen picked at the cuff of her coat. The relaxed person we'd dined with that evening was being replaced by a worried and anxious mother.

"He always seems like a good kid," Mark said.

"He is, I don't know why he hasn't bonded with his sister," Helen said.

Back inside the house, I took Mark in my arms and gave him a kiss. "I've wanted to do that all evening."

"Me, too." Mark returned the kiss, with interest. "Wish there was a gay pub near here."

"We might get a chance to visit one next weekend when we see my Gran."

"We couldn't go out without her while we're there."

"She'd come with us."

"Huh?" Mark didn't understand.

"I'll ask her when we get there, but I bet she'd be up for it."

"Really?"

I smiled. "Gran's a pretty liberated woman."

Mark shook his head. "Sounds like we're in for an interesting weekend."

I laughed. Remembering one of the subjects that had been discussed back at the pub, I said, "There's no point Paul bringing round an estimate to convert the loft. I can't afford it."

"Maybe when I start earning." Mark's continued unemployment bothered him.

I massaged Mark's shoulders. "Something will turn up. Try not to get too stressed about it."

"I know, I just don't like being idle."

"It'll be okay." I yawned. "I don't know about you, but I'm ready for bed."

Mark smiled. "Me, too. But you won't be going to sleep quite yet."

IT WAS AN interesting week at the library. Yes, we do get them. However, the interest was professional rather than bibliographical. Terry Holt, the senior librarian, announced he was taking early retirement. It seemed he and his wife had found the perfect retirement cottage in Scarborough, a tourist seaside town on the east coast.

It didn't take me long to convince myself I should put in for the post. I was pretty confident I'd get an interview. There were a couple of people, including Mary, if she put in for it, who might apply from the branch. I thought I stood a good chance against any local competition. Mary didn't have a degree, and Sally Timpson in Fiction had only just got the junior's position. So I got an application form and spent my lunch break filling it in.

❖

I WAS FIRST out of the library Friday afternoon. I wanted to get home, eat, and catch the bus to Leeds.

"Lucy, I'm home!" I never tired of saying that. "Hope you're all ready to go?"

"I'm all packed."

We each had a bacon sandwich, made sure everything in the house was cleared away, and all the doors and windows were locked. After leaving a key with Paul and Helen, in case of emergencies, we were off.

"That was the seat," Mark said, looking at a bench as we waited in the bus station.

I knew he was referring to the place where he'd sat when he first arrived in town.

"You okay?" I squeezed his elbow.

"I am, now I'm with you."

I wished I could take him in my arms and kiss him. Of course I couldn't, it being a busy thoroughfare in the centre of town. I hope the glance I gave him showed him how much I understood and how much I loved him.

Previously, when I got the bus to Gran's, I would just slump into a corner and pull out a book. However, with the distracting presence of Mark sitting next to me, I kept having to read the same paragraph over and over again. Eventually I closed the book and put it back in my bag.

Mark fared much better. He'd taken the Walkman and was listening to some country and western music. Mark's choice of music was about the only thing we disagreed on. I couldn't stand the noise, but Mark liked it, and had plenty of opportunities to listen to it while I was at work.

We pulled into the central bus station. I directed Mark to the stand where the bus to Gran's was due to leave from.

The bus came, and I started to sit in a seat near the front.

"No," Mark shook his head. "I want to sit at the back. I like to watch people and you can't do that as easily from the front."

This reminded me of a funny story.

"What?" Mark asked.

"I just remembered something Gran told me when she got this bus home once. She sat in front of a couple of women who were having an interesting conversation. Gran got so involved listening to it that she stayed on past her stop. She had to pay the extra fare to the driver, too."

"I've almost done that a couple of times myself," Mark said.

"I haven't, but I once heard a fragment of a conversation on a bus. One old lady said to the other 'but why did she keep it on top of the wardrobe?' I've wondered for years what was kept up there."

Later in the journey Mark asked, "Why did your Gran move from Littleborough to Leeds?"

"The terraced houses she lived in were earmarked for demolition. They grew more and more impossible for the Council to maintain, so she was offered another place on the other side of town. But she decided to move to an old people's community over here instead. She loves it."

"Loads more old ladies to boss around I suppose." Mark chuckled.

"Yeah, I think you're right," I replied.

Looking out of the window, the commercial premises eventually gave way to houses. Some—especially those close to the city—were of poor design and in a bad state of repair. As the bus moved into the suburbs, gradually the quality of the dwellings improved. I signalled to Mark that we were about to reach our stop. We alighted from the bus and began to walk the one hundred yards or so to Gran's place.

"You've spoken to Gran on the phone a few times. She'll no doubt try to make you blush. Don't worry, she's harmless."

"I know, she's already managed to do that, several times," Mark said.

We'd only just crossed her threshold when Gran said, "Mark,

you're even more sexy in the flesh than on the telephone. Simon, get me my little red pills…I feel faint."

"Gran! Leave the poor man alone. And besides, you don't take any red pills."

"He knows I'm only joking. Now, come on in and take off your coats if you're stopping. I imagine you two have been doing the horizontal tango since you met, so I've put you both in the spare room. Though that bed isn't as young as it used to be, so be gentle with it."

"Gran!" I repeated.

"At my age, all I get to do about sex is talk about it."

"I'm sure you're fighting off the men with a stick," Mark said.

"You're such a charmer. If you get tired of Simon, you can move in with me."

Mark reddened again.

"Gran, if you don't behave, we won't take you out tonight," I said.

Her lined face lit up. "Where are we going?"

I wondered if I could actually shock the old dear. "We were thinking about taking you to a gay pub."

"Which one? That new one that just opened up in the centre of the city is very good."

"What?" I asked in amazement.

"I got myself a ticket for their opening night. The drinks were a bit dear, but the male stripper, wow, he didn't half have a big one!"

The old gal had turned the tables on me once again. Mark doubled over when he saw the expression on my face.

"Were you thinking about getting up a visit for the old ladies to go?" Mark asked.

"God, no, half of them would collapse at the mere thought."

Gran bustled round getting us something to eat, and we settled in for entertaining conversation. I felt sure I would die when the baby photos of me came out.

"I thought I burned all those," I said.

"Your mother had a second set. Look, Mark, this is Simon on the hearth rug."

Why do parents insist on taking pictures of their newborn offspring lying naked on a rug? The child isn't old enough to object. The only purpose I could think of was to use the pictures to embarrass them when they grew up.

It got too late to go out that night. I can't say I was disappointed. I'd had a long day at work, and with the bus journey and everything, by the time Gran's mantle clock struck eleven, I was yawning my head off.

"It's time you two young men were in bed," Gran said.

Neither of us disagreed.

MUCH OF SATURDAY was spent helping Gran set up for a dance that would be held at the senior citizen's centre the following day. We broke for lunch and went back to Gran's. She knew how to lay on a good spread.

"Now then you two, tuck in. I don't think we'll have time for a big tea tonight."

"Why?" Mark asked.

Gran gave him a surprised look. "We're going to that nightclub we talked about yesterday, aren't we?"

Nightclub? I shivered, remembering the last one I'd visited. "I thought we were going to a gay pub," I said, picturing a quiet, country-style pub, horse-brasses hanging on a stone fireplace with logs burning in the grate.

"Yes, nightclub," Gran said. "The new one I visited in the city centre, the one with the expensive drinks and the stripper." She gave me a funny look.

"Oh," was all I could think of to say.

"By the time we've finished moving all those tables at the centre, and got the decorations right, I'll hardly have enough time to get ready, let alone cook a meal."

"Uh." I shot a worried look at Mark, who was facing Gran.

GRAN REALLY DID herself up well that evening. She had a long black evening dress; low at the shoulders, to me it spoke of restrained elegance. With the use of discreet jewellery, she looked fantastic. Mark and I looked positively underdressed by comparison.

Gran drove us into Leeds. I wasn't all that comfortable about getting into a moving vehicle with her behind the wheel. I was sure her eyesight wasn't what it used to be, and she was no stranger to the accelerator pedal either.

Two rather shaken young men and a totally unperturbed senior citizen emerged from the nearby multi-storey car park.

"Gentlemen, are we set to party?" Gran asked.

I nodded, but my insides were in knots. I hadn't exactly enjoyed myself the last time I'd visited a nightclub. However, with Mark at my side, I imagined things would be a good deal easier.

It soon became apparent things weren't easier. The music, which Gran loved, was too loud for me. Men didn't approach me, for which I was grateful, but some showed more than a passing interest in Mark. I couldn't really blame them. But when they just came up to him and began to grind against him, that was when I really became upset. Mark told each one to leave him alone, but it wasn't long before another would come along. The difference in how he and I were treated began to make me feel more and more inadequate. I saw how good looking many of the men were, and catching a glimpse of my reflection in a mirror, I realised Mark could do much better than me.

"You okay?" Mark shouted in my ear.

I nodded, determined not to spoil Mark's night out. I even managed to find a smile from somewhere. "You enjoying it?"

Mark shrugged. "It's a bit packed in here."

I nodded in agreement, the place was pretty full.

We had another drink and I forced myself to take a turn on the dance floor, but I was getting a headache and was finding it harder and harder to hide my discomfort.

Gran was also on the dance-floor, showing a group of young men some moves to the song that was currently playing. Mark must have left me, because I saw him approach her, bend, and say something in her ear. She looked in my direction, nodded at Mark, then approached me.

Taking my arm, Gran said, "You're not enjoying yourself."

I denied it, but Gran was having none of it as she led me to the nearest exit.

Once out on the street, I said, "You and Gran go back in. I'll have a cup of coffee over there." I pointed to a café on the other side of the road. "It isn't fair that I spoil your night out, god knows we don't get many of them."

Mark shook his head. "You weren't enjoying yourself, and I wasn't all that happy about being felt up."

Despite what Mark said, I felt dreadful for being a wet blanket and spoiling his evening. "I don't deserve someone as understanding as you. I've told you before I'm such a stick-in-the-mud. You're probably better off finding someone else…"

"Stop it, and stop it right now!" Mark was angry, I'd never seen him so worked up. "I love you. I love you for what you are, not for the kind of nightlife you like. I've told you before, you are absolutely the best thing that has ever happened to me." Softening his tone, and kissing me briefly on the lips, he said, "Got that?"

Mark opened his arms and I fell into them.

"You're the best thing that's ever happened to me, too," I said quietly into his neck.

Gran put a hand on each of our shoulders. "I've watched you two pretty closely while you've been staying with me. Simon, I know things haven't been easy for you. And I bet you've had a few painful times, too, Mark. I've been around a long time, and

I've seen a lot. You two need each other." Buttoning her coat, she said, "And now I've said my piece, I'll shut up."

We both gave Gran a big hug.

The ride back to Gran's was quiet. I sat in the back seat with Mark, my head on his shoulder. Even Gran seemed to sense the mood and drove quite sedately.

When we got into bed, Mark spooned me and put his strong arms around me.

Some time later, Mark whispered, "Can't sleep?"

"No, angel."

He kissed the back of my neck. "Feeling any better about tonight?"

I sniffed. "Not much. I heard what you said outside the club, but…" I sniffed again, "Any one of those good-looking men tonight would have…Sorry. I know I'm being stupid."

"How many nights have you comforted me? How many evenings have you sat and listened to me pour out my troubles? What I'm saying is, I'm here for you this time. I love you, and only you. I've needed to lean on you so much in the past, but you know, you can lean on me, too."

I turned round, and despite the almost total darkness, immediately found Mark's lips. "I hated it in that place. I'm used to not attracting anyone's attention…but it got too much when everyone seemed interested in you. It brought home to me how different we are, and how much better you could do for yourself." I put a finger on Mark's lips. "I know I'm being silly, I know you love me…and I love you. But when you've spent a lifetime being regarded as a lesser person because of how you look, you eventually begin to believe that you are a lesser person."

"Simon."

Shaking my head, I said, "I know. I try to fight my feelings of inadequacy as much as I can, and believe me, having you in my life has helped more than you'll ever know. But there are times when it gets too much."

"And those times are when you come to me." Mark kissed

me and pulled me closer to him. "I don't know why you chose to go to such a place if they make you feel so uncomfortable."

"I didn't." I told Mark about what I'd had in mind.

"Why didn't you say anything?"

"Because Gran was looking forward to going to a nightclub, and I thought maybe it'd be all right this time because I'd be with you."

Mark sighed. "I wish you'd have said something."

"Me, too."

"Come here." Mark began a series of slow kisses that soon had me forgetting all about the nightclub, its patrons, heck, before he'd finished I was having difficulties remembering my own name.

Chapter 3

SUNDAY, GRAN WAS on the tail of the caterers who were providing food for the dance at the centre that night. Mark and I felt we were in the way. Or rather, I wanted to get out of the way. Gran—when she was in full organisation mode—was a force to be reckoned with.

"You know, if you had a second bedroom in that house, I could come and visit you," she said as we were getting ready to leave that morning. "It isn't fair for you to always come over here, and I've got friends back home, and…"

Mark raised his eyebrows at me.

"Funny you should mention that, 'cause…" I told Gran about the plans Paul had drawn up.

"Is he a good builder?" she asked.

"The Council put in tenders for the library extension. They didn't just go on price, but on proven performance, too. Paul got the contract. We only had a minor fault show up a few months after Paul had finished, but he came back and fixed it without any fuss."

After being told how much Paul was charging for the job and assuring herself it was a fair price, Gran got to her feet and began searching the top drawer of her writing desk.

"Here it is." She pulled out her cheque book and wrote in it. Tearing off the cheque she handed it to me. "Put this into your bank account."

I looked at the cheque; it was for the full amount.

"Gran, we can't take this, it's too much."

"I've told you before, you'll get most of my money when the good lord takes me. Your mum and dad are comfortably settled. I want to see you settled as well. Anyway, as I said, I'd like to spend time with you and my friends. Just make sure the staircase he puts in isn't too steep, my old bones aren't up to scaling Mount Everest."

"You are one amazing lady," Mark said.

"I'm glad you've finally realised that," Gran said, a twinkle in her eye, but I could tell she was touched by Mark's words. "Now, be gone with the pair of you. The buses on a Sunday aren't reliable, and I've got to make sure those dim-witted caterers don't balls up this do I've been landed with organising."

"Admit it, Gran, you'd be bored out of your mind if you weren't organising something."

"Yes, you're probably right." Unable to stay serious for long, Gran followed up with, "Now bugger off, otherwise you'll miss that bus."

With the light traffic, and few passengers, we made good time home.

After a restorative cup of coffee, Mark asked, "Can we nip round to Paul's and see when he can start on the loft?" Clearly

Gran had won over another convert. This was confirmed when he added, "I got tired just watching your Gran in action. You know she did just as much work as we did yesterday at the centre."

"I know. I've told you before, I'm much closer emotionally to Gran than any other member of my family. She's been a rock for me for as long as I can remember."

We walked round to the Bates house.

"Would you two like a cuppa?" Helen asked when she let us in.

"No, thanks," Mark said. "We had one just a few minutes ago."

Paul walked down the hallway. "He wouldn't even bring these dirty cot sheets downstairs." He came into the room and saw us. "Sorry, guys, didn't know you were here."

"Hi, Paul," Mark said.

"You had a good time in Leeds?" Paul put the dirty laundry on the floor next to the washing machine.

"Yes, all in all it was a good weekend." I pushed away the unpleasant images of the nightclub.

"That's good." Paul opened the door in the front of the washing machine and started to load it.

"Sam still not co-operating with the baby?" Mark nodded at the dirty laundry.

"He pretends she doesn't exist," Helen said.

"And what doesn't exist can't dirty sheets and blankets." Paul shook his head.

"Oh dear." I sympathised. Knowing there was little else I could do, I said, "Sorry for interrupting your Sunday, but we've come to offer you the job for the loft conversion. Gran says she wants to use the room when she visits."

"That's great. Hang on a tick." Paul left the kitchen.

Helen finished loading the washing machine, added powder and fabric conditioner then started it up.

"Sorry, love," Paul said, coming back, "I'd have done that."

Helen smiled. "It's okay."

Paul laid a large black diary on the table. After inviting us to take a seat, he began to leaf through the pages. "Yeah, I had a cancellation. Bloody Jill Pearce decided she didn't want a raised patio anymore. I told her it wouldn't look right, but she said it would and made me book the time. Fortunately I didn't buy the materials. She rang late last week to say I was right, she'd have the garden turfed instead. So, how does this Wednesday sound?"

"That soon?" Mark asked.

"I told you there wasn't much going on this time of year. But in the summer, I have to turn work away."

"Okay, then, Wednesday it is," I said. "Look, we've nothing much on, do you think Sam would like to come back with us for a bit."

"I'm sure he'll jump at the chance," Helen said. She was right.

Back at our house we got Sam sat down and fed him a few sandwiches.

Mark sat on the sofa opposite Sam in the chair. "What's all this about you ignoring Charlotte?"

"She's a pain."

"How do you mean?" I sat next to Mark and took his hand.

"She just cries, sleeps, cries again, craps her nappy, cries some more and drinks milk."

"She's a baby. I'm sure you did exactly the same when you were that age." I smiled at him.

"I bet I didn't cry as much."

"If she had a loving brother who looked after her, perhaps she wouldn't cry as much," Mark said.

"I wish she was a boy."

"Why's that?" I asked.

"Because when she gets older, all she'll want to do is play with dolls and things."

"Not necessarily," I put in. "The girl who used to live next door to me when I was growing up didn't play with dolls. She would climb trees, kick a football around, and she was an absolute demon at marbles." I didn't add that she also picked fights with the boys, and generally won them. "She was just like the other boys."

"Yeah, but Charlotte…it's such a girly name."

"It's a nice name," Mark said. "And she isn't responsible for her name, is she?"

"No, but I wanted a brother, someone I could mess about with, be friends with, you know, share secrets and stuff like that."

"Think about it. Why can't you do those things with a sister?" Mark said.

"I don't like girls."

"Oh?" I asked. "You might when you get older."

He shook his head then looked at us both, staring at our joined hands. "I think I'm gay," he said in a quiet voice.

I smiled. "It's possible you might be, but you're still only fourteen, it might be too early to know for sure."

"When did you know? About yourself I mean?"

I should have predicted that would be his next question. "About your age," I conceded.

"Me, too," Mark added. "But Simon's right, you still might not know for sure that you're gay."

"But I like spending my time with other boys my age. And when I come round here, it's…" Sam seemed to struggle for the right words. "It's comfortable. I can be myself."

"Well, young man," I said, thinking it was high time we lightened the mood, "It just so happens that your dad will be converting our loft into a bedroom starting this Wednesday."

"Wow!" Sam perked up immediately. "Can I come and live with you both?"

"No!" Both Mark and I said at the same time.

Sam's face fell. "I thought you liked me coming round."

"We do," I said. "But coming round and living here are two different things. You have a home, and parents who love you very much, and anyway, that room is for my Gran and my parents when they want to come and visit. But,"—I paused for dramatic effect—"I can't see why you can't come stay for the odd weekend."

"Cool!" Sam stood and began to walk around.

"But only if your mum and dad say it's okay," I added, realising I should have made that condition clearer sooner.

"And if you don't help out more with the baby they might say no," Mark put in.

"You guys are great." Sam treated us to a broad smile. "I knew you'd be all right about me being gay and everything."

"We know what it's like." Mark put a hand on Sam's shoulder. "Have you told your mum and dad that you think you might be gay?"

"Yeah, they're all right about it, but like you they think I'm too young to know for sure."

Mark patted Sam's shoulder. "If you are gay, then it'll be up to Charlotte to give them grandkids."

Sam giggled.

"All the more reason for you to be nice to her then," I said.

"Okay, okay, I'll try and be a better brother."

We both gave him a big hug. Sam really responded well to physical contact.

"WHAT DID YOU say to Sam yesterday?" Paul asked me in the street Monday afternoon.

"Why?" I wondered if I should start to worry.

"He offered to change a dirty nappy this morning, Helen tells me."

I breathed more easily. "We told him that if he was a good boy, and if you and Helen agreed, we would let him spend the odd night in the new bedroom. You wouldn't mind, would you?"

"Not at all." Paul shook his head. "You two are working miracles with that boy. Erm, Simon, I guess he's told you that he thinks he's gay."

I nodded. "He seems pretty certain about it."

"Sorry if this is too personal a question, but—"

"Did I know at his age if I was gay?"

Paul nodded.

"I knew. But different people realise it at different ages." Feeling I ought to bring something up sooner rather than later, I said, "Mark and I…we could never, would never, do anything…inappropriate with Sam. I just thought with him staying over I should—"

"If I had the slightest doubt Sam would be put in danger, I wouldn't have left him with you when Charlotte was born." Paul put a large, work-roughened hand on my shoulder. "I trust you two completely."

"Thanks, Paul, that means a lot. It's not easy to gain acceptance. People don't understand, and it's human nature to reject things they don't understand."

"I know. Helen's parents have never come to terms with the fact their son Steve is gay. I try and avoid the subject with them when we visit because it makes me so angry they could be like that to their own flesh and blood."

I sighed. "Sadly, it happens all too often."

"I can promise you it won't happen with Sam. Helen and I love that boy, and nothing will change that."

"I hope he realises that he's a very lucky boy. My mum and dad are just about okay with my sexuality. They know I'm close to Mark, but they haven't asked for details, so I haven't given them any."

"Sorry to hear that."

I shrugged.

Sighing, Paul said, "Well, I better get to the builder's yard before they close. Got a job starting Wednesday, you know." He winked.

IN THE PAST, I'd never had much difficulty getting up for work. However, that was in the pre-Mark days. Now it was sheer torture to have to leave his warm, slightly furry and eminently huggable body of a morning. Mark wanted to get up with me, but I told him there really wasn't any point. He might as well stay under the quilt where it was warm. I was beginning to worry about him though. Not being able to find work was really getting to him. He felt humiliated having to sign on as unemployed every two weeks.

When I arrived at work, I found a message in my pigeonhole. I'd landed an interview for the senior's position.

I gave Mary a hug when she told me she'd received a rejection letter. "You'd have knocked 'em dead if they'd have given you a chance," I told her.

"You're a sweetheart." She kissed my cheek. "I'm not sure I would have wanted the extra responsibility, anyway. Plus there'd be a lot more paper shuffling."

I knew. I had to admit it bothered me that I wouldn't get as much contact with the public. The job, if I got it, would be meetings, paper shuffling, as Mary said, costing proposals, report writing, and the like. Not as interesting at first glance, but I was sure I'd find something in that lot to get my teeth into. And of course the money would be better.

As I predicted, Sally Timpson didn't get an interview either. She told me later she was secretly glad as she hadn't yet got to grips with the job she was doing. Although I knew in a few years' time she'd start climbing the promotional ladder and would probably overtake me.

The aura of good luck stayed with me for the rest of the day. What with one thing and another I was running late at lunchtime, so I nipped down the street to Daphne's for a quick sandwich and cup of coffee. Daphne herself was cleaning tables and waiting on customers. She normally stayed in the kitchen or behind the counter. Belinda—her usual help—seemed not to be around.

"Bel on holiday today?" I asked.

Daphne looked up from wiping a nearby table. "She gave in her notice this morning, and as she was owed a couple of weeks' holiday, she left straight away. Something to do with family problems. She didn't say, and frankly I wasn't interested."

I raised an eyebrow. Daphne had never spoken about her staff like this before. I was about to say as much when she continued.

"Bel's work had taken a nosedive recently. She'd been mooning over a boy, but he wasn't interested in her. If I'd heard another tale of unrequited love, I swear I'd have..." Daphne shook her head and moved onto another table. "I'll have to go down to the job centre. It's near impossible to get good, honest staff with experience, and frankly I haven't the time to look through applications, hold interviews and the rest."

"Sorry. Can I use your phone for a minute? It's only a local call."

"Go ahead." She waved her cloth at the phone on the counter and got back to her table cleaning.

"I might be able to fix you up with someone. You remember Mark, my...boyfriend?" Daphne had worked out what Mark meant to me the first time she saw the two of us.

She nodded and picked up a tray of dirty plates.

"I know he used to work in a café up in Newcastle," I told her. "I'll give him a ring to see if he can come see you."

"I'll interview him straight away."

I smiled.

"Thanks, love." She returned my smile and took the tray into the back.

Unfortunately, my shortened lunch break meant I was leaving the café as Mark was entering it. I briefly told him not to hide anything about his background, even though it was a painful subject. Knowing Daphne as long as I had, I knew she placed a high regard on her staff's honesty.

I WAS SORTING through a pile of returned books when a long-faced Mark came into the department. Sensing the need for privacy, I showed him into the storeroom.

"I'm sorry. I shouldn't have insisted you tell Daphne about your past. One day I'll learn to keep my big mouth shut."

Mark kissed me and gave me a tight hug. "I got it!"

"What? Really? You sod, you had me worried."

"Daphne already knew about…what I'd had to do, and was pleased that I'd owned up."

I nodded.

"I told her that I was honest and hard working. I gave her the phone number of the café I'd worked at in Newcastle. She rang them, and they remembered me and said good things about me."

"That's great."

"Yeah. Daphne said I could start next Monday. I asked her if she needed anyone now. She did, so I start tomorrow at half past seven."

"Wow, that's early."

"I have to give Daphne a hand with the food deliveries. I finish at three in the afternoon, though."

"I won't get as much cuddle time in the mornings," I pouted.

"But the extra money will make up for it."

Squeezing him, I said, "Your cuddles are priceless."

Mark smiled and shook his head.

Sighing, I said, "I better get back to work."

"I'll see you tonight." Mark kissed me, then ran his hands down my sides. "Love you."

I kissed him back. "Love you more."

I DROPPED OFF a key at Paul's on Tuesday night, as Mark wouldn't be there in the morning to let Paul and his crew in to start the loft conversion.

Because of the good news Mark had received, I was no longer worried about telling him I was going for promotion.

"You silly man," Mark said after I'd given him my news.

"You could have told me about it straight away."

"I know, I just didn't want to rub it in."

"I wouldn't have minded. I'd have been happy for you."

I LEARNED THE next day that I'd have to work late on Saturday. We had to prepare a report on what we would like renewed or replaced in the department. The final decision on the allocation of funds wouldn't be made until the start of the new financial year in early April. I was the more senior librarian in non-fiction, so the job fell to me. It was my turn to work the Saturday morning shift, so I just planned to stay all day, and possibly into the evening. I wasn't overly thrilled at the prospect because it was Valentine's Day. In the past I'd have welcomed the distraction. However, I now had Mark. I wanted to be with him for as much of the day as possible.

Mind you, Mark would have to work his usual shift at the café, so it didn't matter too much that I was also working.

I woke Saturday morning alone, Mark having already got up and gone to work. I left his Valentine card on the kitchen table. He'd see it when he came home in the afternoon. I'd only ever bought one other Valentine card in my life. That was for Patrick. Later that week he'd told me he'd received two cards. He'd suspected one had come from a girl he'd had his eye on for a while but had no idea who'd sent the other. Trying to keep my feelings hidden, I'd told him it probably wasn't that important anyway.

I had a momentary pang of sadness when I realised Mark hadn't left a card for me. I didn't know what he felt about the whole Valentine's thing as we hadn't talked about it. With the demands of his new job, perhaps it had slipped his mind.

I'll get a bottle of wine on the way home tonight, I thought as I left the house for work.

THE DAY WENT by with agonising slowness. Maybe an office job would have more appeal after all. Apart from the hour I took for lunch after the library closed to the public, when I managed to get a brief word with Mark, I spent the whole day in the department.

Mark was doing well at the café. It amazed me how he managed to squeeze himself into the tight black trousers Daphne gave him. Daphne claimed the number of female visitors to the café increased, once word got around.

Though, as she said, "Little do the girls realise what a hopeless cause Mark is for them."

I got my budget report finished by six. The key was to ask for double what you actually wanted, such as new books, replacement of worn and tatty books, new equipment, requests for re-decoration etc. Because once the pen pushers at the town hall had whittled away at the report, they would have cut your demands down by about half. So hopefully you'd end up with what you wanted in the first place. The usual rumours did the rounds about how the budget for the next financial year would be even tighter than normal.

It was bitterly cold outside, and rain was threatening. I wound my scarf around my neck and headed for the supermarket for a bottle of wine.

A wrapped bottle of Burgundy safely under my arm, I hazarded the cold outdoors again. The promised rain had arrived, so it was a cold, damp, and miserable Simon who entered through the front door that evening. I didn't even feel like calling out my usual greeting.

The living room was in semi-darkness, the only light coming from the fire. Perhaps Mark had gone out, not knowing what time I'd be back. I switched on the light, hung up my wet coat and made for the kitchen, wine in hand. I hadn't spotted it earlier, but a soft glow was coming from the slightly opened kitchen door. Puzzled, I pushed the door open and entered.

The sight that greeted me knocked me for six. The table

had a red cloth on it, on which stood four candles, the only source of light in the room. The table was set with the best china and a number of serving bowls on the worktop opposite. Mark stood at the far end of the room. He was wearing his café uniform, but had added a black bow tie.

I was at a loss for words.

Mark walked towards me and handed me an envelope. "Happy Valentine's Day."

"How, why, I didn't think… Oh heck…" I sniffed.

"Remember all those meals you cooked for me before I moved in, and all the meals you fed to me when I couldn't use my hands?

I nodded.

"This is a thank you for all those times."

"No one has ever done anything like this for me before." I shook my head. "I haven't ever received a Valentine's card before." I opened the envelope and opened the card. "Thank you, angel." I sniffed again.

Mark switched on the tape recorder, and it began to softly play classical music. I don't know what happened to the bottle of wine, Mark must have taken it from me at some point. He led me over to the table, pulled the chair out, and I sat.

"I hope all your customers at the café don't get this level of service?" I tried to joke.

"Only the very special ones," he replied, kissing my forehead. "Now I'm going to feed you this time, you can feed me as well if you like."

"Uh, okay," I smiled.

Mark uncovered one of the serving dishes. "I had to choose a cold menu because I didn't know what time you'd be home."

That night he served all my favourites. Prawns, which he insisted on peeling for me. Smoked salmon moose, and oysters on the half shell. We finished with cheese, crackers and grapes.

After the meal, Mark wanted to do the washing up by himself. "Remember when I first used to visit…you wouldn't let me help you clean up? Well, you're going to sit there and not lift a finger."

"Mark, the only reason why I wouldn't let you wash up back then was that I had to do something when you'd gone, otherwise I'd have gone mad. I used to clean the place from top to bottom after your visits, just so I wasn't thinking about the wonderful time I'd just had."

Mark came over and we hugged and exchanged a few kisses before he rolled up his sleeves and began the washing up.

THE DAY OF my interview finally arrived. I wasn't nervous because I knew I had a fair chance. Local government being the gossip-ridden place it was, news of who the other candidates were soon filtered out. It was a constant source of amazement to me how quickly news spread in such an organisation.

My interview was at the town hall. I donned my rarely used suit; the last time it had been worn was for the wedding of a distant cousin.

I knew two of the people on the interview panel: the personnel lady from the Council and Mr Gordon, the chief librarian for the district. The other man I didn't know, but he didn't ask many questions.

At the end of the interview they if I had any questions. I hadn't, so Mr Gordon told me that they'd make their decision the next day. I'd be contacted by phone by a member of the interview panel.

I spent the rest of that afternoon looking round the shops. Mark met me after he finished work at 3 pm and suggested we go out for tea in a restaurant. I didn't want to do that. Firstly Mark had seen enough of the inside of eating establishments; also I was too wound up to eat anything.

We decided to go to the cinema, although I didn't take in much of the film. I was replaying the interview in my mind, worrying that my suggestions for raising money for library services were too off-the-wall.

"Stop thinking about it." Mark took hold of my hand and gave it a squeeze. "I'm sure you were great."

I squeezed his hand back in gratitude.

EVERY TIME THE phone rang the next day I jumped up to answer it before the first ring had stopped. This amused Mary no end.

By lunchtime, and with still no call, I convinced myself I hadn't got the job, as they'd tell the successful candidate first, and ask him or her if they actually wanted the post. I wondered why a candidate would go for interview if they didn't want the job in the first place. I decided I'd take my lunch into the reading room. No one was supposed to eat in there, but so long as the readers didn't get the books dirty, Mary and I tended to look the other way.

I'd taken sandwiches; Mark—bless his heart—had made them for me before leaving for work. I didn't feel much like eating, so I shared my lunch with Fred, the town tramp. He'd installed himself by the radiator as usual. I'd just gotten into a very interesting discussion as to why the Germans weren't expecting the D-Day landings in Normandy when Mary poked her head round the door to say there was a phone call for me.

I got up from the table so fast I knocked over my chair. I moved quickly to pick it up and then almost ran for the door.

Mary put her arms out to block the way. "Slow down and take a deep breath."

I did and it helped a little. Mary allowed me through. I approached the phone, praying all the way. A little voice told me it was a bit late now to ask for help from above.

I picked up the receiver. "Hello, Simon Peters here."

"Simon, this is Frank Appleyard, I was on the panel yesterday, and we interviewed you for the post of…" He rambled on. Mr Appleyard was the guy on the panel I didn't know, but I knew who he was now and why he was calling. *Why doesn't he get on with it?* I gritted my teeth. "…Senior Librarian, I'm sorry…"

Because he's calling me, rather than the chief librarian, it means I didn't get it.

"…Simon, are you still there?"

"Huh? Sorry, Mr Appleyard, I didn't catch what you said, there must be a fault on the line." I was proud of myself for coming up with that one so quickly.

He chuckled. "On behalf of the interview panel I would like to offer you the post of Senior librarian at the Littleborough Branch."

My mouth opened, but nothing came out.

"Will you accept the post?"

"Thank you, yes, Mr Appleyard, I accept!"

"Excellent."

"Thank you. But I was confused as to why you had begun the conversation by saying that you were sorry."

He laughed. "Yes, I was apologising for the fact that Mr Gordon had fallen ill last night, and because of that it took longer than we would have liked to get back to you with our decision."

"Okay." I also laughed. Then I realised my amusement might be interpreted as insensitive to the Chief's condition. "Sorry, is Mr Gordon feeling better now?"

"He was able to come in about an hour ago."

"That's good."

"We'll post a written confirmation of our offer. If you could get it back to us as soon as possible, then Personnel can do their thing."

"Thank you, Mr Appleyard, for letting me know."

"You're welcome. Oh, and Simon? Maybe the first thing you should do when you start your new job is to have the phone system checked." He laughed.

"Yes, I will, sir, thank you." I also laughed.

After putting the phone down, I spotted Mary hovering nearby. "I got it!"

"Yes!" she shouted.

"Shhhh," I said, looking round at the few bemused members of the public who were staring at Mary.

"Sorry," she whispered.

I related the strange conversation I'd had with Mr Appleyard.

"You daft bugger." She shook her head in amusement.

"I know my lunch is almost up, but would you mind if I nipped out to Daphne's and told Mark?"

"Course not." Mary waved me away. As I was leaving I heard her add, "boss."

WALKING DOWN THE street, I thought I might do the same trick that Mark had pulled on me. But I just couldn't wipe the silly grin off my face. Mark must have been watching the door, because as soon as I walked through it, he saw my face, asked Daphne if he could take me into the back and motioned me into a storage room off the kitchen.

"Congratulations." He hugged me and gave me a kiss. "You deserve that promotion."

"Thanks, I didn't think they were going to give it to me." I told him what had happened during the morning.

He laughed. "You silly bugger."

"Mary said pretty much the same thing."

"Yeah, I bet she did. Listen, do you want to go out tonight and celebrate?"

Grinning, I said, "I'd rather stay in and celebrate."

Chapter 4

"DO WE GET a ribbon to cut like they have on those home makeover programmes on the telly?" Mark asked when Paul proclaimed the new bedroom finished.

"You daft sod." Paul shook his head.

Ascending the two flights of stairs behind Paul, I had to admit the man looked really sexy in his tight jeans and tool belt. A poke from behind by Mark soon got my mind back to the new room rather than the person who had built it.

Paul and his crew had been remarkably tidy during the past week, cleaning up after themselves at the end of each day. I wondered if that was Helen's influence.

Of course we'd watched each phase of the conversion pretty closely, but it was great to finally see the finished article.

"As we agreed, the skylight has patterned glass in it for privacy." Paul pointed up at the ceiling. "Not that anyone could really see in. It faces west, so anyone sleeping in here won't be bothered by strong sunlight in the morning."

"Good idea," Mark said, impressed.

Paul bowed. "There's a light switch by the door, and a pull cord over here," he walked along one wall. "So it'd be best to have the head of the bed about here."

Mark and I nodded.

"There are mains sockets near where the bed should be for electric clocks, bedside lamps, that sort of thing. There's also a socket on the opposite wall. The roof has been insulated, and the old insulation that would have been beneath your feet has been removed. It wasn't thick enough anyway. The water tanks and other pipes are behind that wall. There's a hidden door, so you can get to them if you need to. I've lagged them. If we got a cold snap, you might have had frozen pipes. Last, but not least," Paul walked to the opposite wall, "a double radiator. It'll probably get cold up here."

"Thanks, Paul," I said. "I've got the cash out of the bank as you asked."

Paying with cash meant we could avoid Value Added Tax on some of the work. A bit naughty, but it saved some money.

Gran had rung up a few days earlier to check on how the work was coming along. When she'd been told it was almost done, she'd surprised me by saying she was sending more money.

"Why?" I asked.

"You don't expect me to sleep on bare boards in an undecorated room do you?"

"No, Gran, 'course not." The truth was everything had happened so fast I hadn't given that much thought to buying a carpet, paint and a bed.

❖

MARK AND I decided to decorate the room ourselves. I took the remainder of my leave from work so I could get the project finished. As the walls were new plasterboard it seemed pointless to paper over them, so we just put on a couple of coats of emulsion paint in a warm pastel shade. The woodwork was done in a plain white gloss.

We chose a brown carpet with gold threads and a double bed. Gran had been generous, so I was able to get a couple of bedside tables, lamps, a wardrobe and a chest of drawers. Finally came pillows and a duvet plus a couple of changes of sheets.

When the room was finally set up, Mark and I fell onto the bed.

"Want to christen it?" Mark waggled his eyebrows.

"Should we?"

"Would your Gran object?"

We thought for a moment then burst out laughing and helped each other out of our clothes.

THE NEXT DAY was a Saturday, and one of Mark's weekends off. We'd just finished breakfast when we heard someone knocking on the front door. Mark went to answer.

"Come in."

"Just thought I'd pop round," Sam said as he and Mark entered the kitchen.

"Want a cuppa?" I stood. I'd bought teabags especially for Sam and any other visitor who didn't like coffee.

"It's okay thanks, just had one at home."

"How's home at the moment?" Mark asked. "Still getting along with your baby sister?"

"She's okay, I suppose." Sam examined his shoes momentarily, then looked up and said, "I know my dad has finished the new bedroom, and I saw a bed being delivered here yesterday. I wondered if I could go and have a look?"

"Ah, so that's the real reason for you coming round," I teased.

Sam laughed. "Well…I came to see you two as well, of course."

"Of course." Mark turned to me. "Shall we let him look?"

"Well, I don't know." I scratched my chin. "Gran did say she wanted to be the first to see it."

Sam's face began to fall.

"But I don't think she'd mind if I let you have a look."

Sam shot out of the kitchen and up the stairs. We followed at a more leisurely pace.

"It's great. I like the colour scheme, it's really warm," Sam enthused.

"Okay, you can sleep here if your parents agree." I knew he was about to ask us if he could stay, so I thought I'd save him the trouble.

"Can I?"

"Only if your mum and dad agree," Mark added.

"They will."

I knew they'd have an unhappy teenager on their hands if they didn't.

"What about making it a guy's night in?" I asked. "Having a pizza delivered, watching a video and all that?"

"Can I have some beer?" Sam's eyes twinkled.

"No!" Mark and I said together.

"It was worth a try," Sam smirked.

"You'll discover the pleasures, and problems, of alcohol soon enough," I said.

He nodded.

I was sure I was coming across like an old fart.

"Okay if I come round at about six?"

"We want to hear from one of your parents first," Mark reminded him.

"EITHER WE'VE GOT a hungry burglar, or Sam is cooking us breakfast." Mark yawned.

"Huh?" I opened my eyes.

"By the smell of it, Sam is cooking us breakfast."

It was my turn to yawn. "I suppose we better make a move." I didn't want to: Mark and I didn't get many opportunities to stay in bed in the morning.

"Suppose." Mark rubbed his eyes. "This must be one of the downsides of having kids."

Sam had indeed cooked us breakfast. The kitchen table was set, complete with paper napkins and glasses of orange juice. A pot of real coffee was brewing in the machine.

"I'm glad you're up. It'll only be a few more minutes," Sam said.

"Wow, mate," Mark said.

"I wanted to thank you both for having me over."

"With service like this, you can come anytime," I said.

"Really? Can I?"

"Well, yes, but don't forget that bedroom is also for Simon's Gran, or his mum and dad. And what about your parents? I'm sure they'd want to be reminded every now and again that their only begotten son was still alive."

He laughed. "Yeah, they're not too bad, I suppose."

"I think that's what's known as being damned by faint praise," I said.

We ate the breakfast Sam had prepared. He'd made a first class job of it, and Mark and I were not slow to pass on our compliments either.

"Now, as you made the breakfast, it's up to Simon and me to do the washing up."

"I don't mind doing it, honestly," Sam said.

"Good grief," Mark turned to me. "Is this child for real? Quick, Simon, sneak round the back of him to see if you can see any stray wires, the Sam that we tucked up into bed last night has been replaced by an android."

Sam giggled.

"Well, whoever you are, you're not doing the washing up.

Sit in the living room and watch the telly or something."

Sam did as he was told, and Mark and I cleaned up the kitchen. Sam had been very tidy; most kids his age, if they'd have thought about making breakfast at all, would have used every pot and pan in the place.

SAM'S FACE FELL when we told him that Mark and I were going out and maybe he should go back home and spend some time with his family.

"Can't I stop with you two for a bit longer? Or are you going somewhere private?"

I explained that Mark and I usually went for a walk on a Sunday morning if the weather was decent.

"I suppose you could tag along if you wanted, but I don't want you complaining you're bored ten minutes in," Mark said, looking at me for my agreement.

I nodded. "We usually go to the pub for a drink afterward, though."

"No problem." Sam beamed at being included.

"We'll have to sit in the children's room, I don't want Ron losing his licence."

"That's okay, Mum and Dad sometimes take me and we sit in there. We can have a game of table soccer if you like."

"Yeah, mate, that's a good idea," Mark said.

"And I'll play the winner then," I offered.

AS WE HADN'T visited the woods for a while, we decided to go there. Sam raced ahead of us and played hide and seek, but he was so excited, constantly giggling, he was too easy to find. Not that this bothered him in the least. After Mark and I had walked far enough—Sam must have covered at least three times the distance with his constant running around—we headed towards the Mucky Duck.

Sam made a half-hearted attempt at wanting a beer, but we told him he couldn't.

"Have you actually tasted it?" I asked.

"No, but Mum and Dad let me have shandy," he grinned.

"Would you like a shandy this time?" Mark patted his pocket, probably to check to see he had his wallet.

"Please," Sam said.

When Mark had left the children's room for the public bar, I asked Sam if he would like to take a small sip of my beer when it came. I told him he'd have to be careful not to let anyone see though.

"Ace! I bet Dad would let me, but Mum always says no."

"It'll have to remain a secret between ourselves then. Though I suppose you could tell your dad."

Mark came back with the drinks and Sam took a small sip of my pint.

"Yuck! It's strong!"

"I thought you'd say that," I chuckled. "You'll probably grow to like the taste as you get older though. I didn't much like beer at your age."

Mark had stayed quiet through all this, then said, "When you get older treat drink with respect. Don't overdo it."

Sam gave Mark a puzzled look.

"My dad's an alcoholic, and he gets pretty nasty when he drinks."

Sam shivered. "I promise I'll take it easy."

The fact Mark usually joked around with Sam probably helped the teenager understand how serious Mark was being.

"Good lad." Mark seemed to snap out of his melancholy. "Now what's this about you wanting to thrash me at table soccer?"

We enjoyed a fun couple of hours in the pub. I think Mark let Sam beat him at the soccer game. I knew I wasn't much good at it, so it didn't take Sam long to wipe the floor with me.

"I'm the champion!" Sam declared once the mini-tournament was over.

"I guess we better head back now. Your mum and dad might think we've kidnapped you," Mark said.

"Suppose."

I could see Sam was disappointed. "Tell you what," I said. "I'll be talking to my Gran in the week, and if she isn't coming next weekend, then how's about you stopping over again?"

Sam brightened.

Our happy group left the pub and made its way home. We walked three abreast, Sam in the middle, chatting away, pointing at various things. Mark didn't know Littleborough as well as Sam and I, who had both grown up here.

"You see that cracked pane of glass, in the next to the bottom window in the telephone box?" Sam asked.

Mark nodded.

"Billy Tranter and me broke it a couple of years ago when we were playing football. We nearly piss…err. I mean we nearly wet ourselves as we ran off."

Mark and I were trying not to laugh at Sam's slip up.

"We're all guys here. I'm not saying that we should use a swear word in every sentence, but sometimes a swear word is the right word to use. Especially when you're frightened, and you think you might…piss yourself," I told Sam.

"You two are so cool. Mum would have me wash my mouth out with soap if I talked about pissing myself."

"And she'd be right, if you said it in front of a woman," Mark said.

As we approached Sam's house I saw Paul in his driveway, washing his van.

"You missed a bit," I joked.

Paul turned round. "Hi, guys."

"Hi, Dad."

"I hope you've been behaving yourself for Mark and Simon?"

"Daaaad! I'm not a little kid."

Paul laughed and mussed his son's hair. "Sorry, couldn't resist teasing you. Did you have a nice time though?"

Sam nodded.

"Okay, go upstairs and change. When I've finished this we're going to visit your granddad and grandma Hawkins for Sunday tea."

"Okay." Sam thanked us for having him, then walked into the house.

"I hope he wasn't any trouble?" Paul asked.

"None at all," I said.

We gave Paul a brief rundown of the events of the past 24 hours. I could tell he was surprised Sam had cooked us breakfast. His surprise quickly turned to pride. I could almost see Paul's chest puff out.

"He really seems to have taken to you two," Paul said.

"And we've really taken to him," Mark replied. "We'd like him to come over sometime next weekend, if that's all right with you."

"No problem." Paul hesitated for a moment. "I'm being really cheeky asking this, and trust me you can say no if it's too much, but..." He squeezed his sponge, causing water to drip onto his white trainers.

"Yeah?" I prompted.

"Helen's been a bit down, you know, since the baby came."

"Sorry, I didn't know that," I said.

"Yeah. The doc said a couple of weeks away in the sun would do her the world of good."

I nodded.

"Business is still a bit slow and Helen is still on maternity leave, but Sam's in school, and we don't want him to miss anything."

"Uh huh," Mark said and then looked at me, his eyebrows raised. I knew what he was asking.

"So we kind of shelved the idea and—"

"Don't shelve it. Go," I said. "We'd be glad to look after

Sam while you were away, wouldn't we?" I turned to Mark who was nodding enthusiastically.

"You sure?" Paul asked.

"'Course we're sure," Mark said. "So long as you bring us back some duty free."

"Mark!" I nudged my boyfriend.

Paul laughed. "Honestly are you sure? It's a lot to ask."

"We're sure." I nodded. "So long as it's okay with Sam, of course."

"I'm sure it will, but let's go ask him." Paul dumped his sponge in his bucket and jogged into the house calling Sam's name.

We followed Paul inside and waited in the hallway as he went upstairs.

"Thanks, Simon." Mark smiled at me.

I touched his cheek. "No problem. Sam's a great kid, he'll be no trouble." I hoped he'd be no trouble, I had precious little experience of dealing with teenagers full-time.

Mark opened his mouth to reply when Sam came barrelling down the stairs, Paul following more slowly.

Crashing into Mark, Sam said, "I couldn't believe it when Dad told me!"

Mark ruffled Sam's hair.

"So I take it the answer's 'yes?'" I smiled down at a grinning Sam.

"It is!"

"You better be on your best behaviour while we're away, I don't want to come home and find that you've been cheeky to Simon and Mark," Paul warned.

"Daaad!" Sam rolled his eyes.

I laughed.

We were shown into the Bates' kitchen, and Helen came downstairs carrying Charlotte. After Mark and I said our helloes to the baby, we sat around the kitchen table and began to discuss a few details of Sam's stay.

"I finish at the Café at three," Mark said. "So I'd be back

when Sam comes home from school."

"Thanks for that," Helen said,

"Though Sam's at an age where we don't mind him being on his own for an hour or two if necessary," Paul added.

I nodded. "Let us know when you've booked the holiday. And we'll talk again."

"And don't forget the bottle of vodka," Mark put in.

I kicked him under the table. "Shut up."

Paul tilted his head back and laughed. "I won't forget."

As time was getting on and I remembered Paul had said they were going to visit Helen's parents, we said our goodbyes and went home.

When we were inside, and he'd wrapped his arms around me, Mark said, "It'll be great to have Sam all to ourselves for a couple of weeks."

"It will, angel. We'll have to think of things we can do to keep him amused and occupied."

Mark nodded. "Though he seems happy enough just hanging around with us."

"That's true. Mark, I've been thinking. Now I've got the promotion, I want to go out and buy a car. I should have no trouble getting it on credit. We can't afford anything flashy, and it would have to be second-hand, but it would be great to have some wheels."

He smiled. "We'd be able to just drive off when we felt like it, and not pore over bus and rail timetables.

I nodded, giving him a squeeze.

"Will you teach me to drive?"

I shook my head. "Giving a partner driving lessons has broken up more relationships than enough."

His face fell.

"Okay, I suppose we could give it a try." I could never say 'no' to Mark.

He kissed me.

"But we're stopping if things don't work out," I insisted.

Mark's smile dimmed a little, but he nodded in agreement.

"I need to go on a refresher course before I start driving. I'll dig out my copy of the *Highway Code*, though I think I remember the important bits."

Mark cupped my groin. "These are the most important bits."

I sighed dramatically. "One track mind."

"Takes one to know one."

I agreed and we raced each other to the bedroom.

AFTER SATISFYING OUR urges, we both lay spent on the bed.

Mark gave me a slow kiss. "Things are really looking up for us. I've got a job, there's your promotion, Sam coming to stay, and now the car. It's all so, so…"

I kissed him back. "I know, my angel. It's perfect." I didn't add that it was Mark being there which made it perfect.

Chapter 5

THE NEXT EVENING Paul hailed me as I passed his house. As we enquired about each other's day, the state of the weather and the economy, I could tell something was on Paul's mind.

"So?" I tilted my head and raised an eyebrow. I'd seen a guy do it in a movie, but I was sure he pulled it off a lot better than I did.

"We've booked a holiday." Paul smiled.

"That's great. Where are you going?"

"Gran Canaria. We fly on Friday from Manchester."

"Wow, so soon?"

"Is that okay?"

"Of course." I waved my hand. "I was just surprised at how fast things were moving. Sam's welcome at our place anytime."

"Our flight is really early Friday morning, so it's up to you if you want to get up early on Friday morning or have him from Thursday evening."

"Thursday evening's fine with us. We generally do the supermarket shopping on a Thursday, and then call in at the Oriental for a take away on the way home. We might as well take Sam to the supermarket so we can buy in some things that he likes, and he can stay and have Chinese with us if that's okay."

"That's a good idea, the supermarket I mean. He eats most things, but is particular about which brand of baked beans he'll eat."

I laughed.

I'd called Gran the day before just to make sure she wasn't planning a visit that would coincide with Sam staying with us.

"So you're already making use of the room?" she'd asked.

I'd explained about Paul and Helen needing to take a holiday.

"And you need the room for their son Sam?"

"Uh huh."

"I've no plans to descend on you, so there's no need to worry on that score."

Gran and I had talked for a few more minutes, then she'd said, "My telly programme's about to start, so..."

I'd laughed. "You and your soap operas. I'll let you go then."

After bidding goodnight to Paul, I walked the few steps home.

Mark was waiting for me in the living room. As we exchanged kisses, his hands wandered under the waistband of my trousers and headed south. Between kisses he asked, "Good day at the office, dear?"

I shook my head and smiled. We were so much the married couple. "Why isn't my dinner on the table?" I waggled my eyebrows.

"Just be a couple more minutes."

"Thanks, angel." Amid yet more kisses I told Mark about seeing Paul and how we'd soon have a houseguest.

"That's great! We'll be able to take him to the supermarket so we can get the sorts of things he likes to eat."

"Great minds think alike." I gave him another kiss. "I said exactly the same thing to Paul."

We had to eat dinner quickly because I'd arranged with Harry Simons—a librarian in the children's section—to come with us to the car auctions that Monday night.

I KNEW VERY little about cars, but Harry was knowledgeable. His brother worked as a mechanic in one of the local repair garages and Harry had picked up quite a bit from him.

Harry was taking us round the cars that would be sold off later that evening. He'd got hold of a copy of the auction catalogue and was checking out the cars that were in our price range.

"You see this?" Harry was running a cloth over the passenger door of a red Ford Escort. He opened the cloth. "This is a magnet. It should stick to the car's bodywork, but see here how it's not sticking?"

Mark and I nodded.

"The car has probably been in an accident, and the owner has used filler to smooth out the dent." He knelt down. "If you look really closely you can see it isn't quite smooth."

"Oh, yeah," I said, kneeling next to Harry.

"So we'll cross this one off the list." Harry ran a black felt tip marker across the listing in the catalogue.

We looked over several cars; each time Harry would check the mileage and a myriad of other details. As time passed, I grew increasingly more pleased that I'd asked him to come along with us to give us the benefit of his experience. Neither Mark nor I would have had a clue. We'd have ended up buying something that quite possibly could have conked out before we'd got it home.

Harry had highlighted a number of vehicles in the catalogue that he thought were worth bidding for.

We made our way to the small tea stand in the auction

room. I was ready for something to drink and, by the looks of them, so were Harry and Mark. Harry had refused to allow me to pay him for his time. The best I could do was to buy the man a large hot chocolate, Mark and I having the same.

"Look, Harry, when it comes to the bidding, would you do it for us? You know what my maximum bid is. I'd be too nervous to do it myself."

Harry chuckled. "No problem."

I got the impression he was secretly pleased I'd asked.

"But you two will have to sit still. You don't want to be putting a bid in yourselves, especially if you're bidding against me."

THE TIME FINALLY came for the auction to start. We went to the bidding area and took our seats.

Looking round, there seemed to be quite a few people present. Harry said many of them were probably dealers. I wondered if so many people meant the price of the cars would go too high for our budget.

The auction began. The cars were driven into the cavernous room and were parked in front of the banked seats where we bidders sat. The auctioneer was in a glass booth facing us on the other side of the roadway, talking into a public address system so he could be heard above the noise of the car engines.

I began to fidget, Harry hadn't raised his hand once, and the auction had been going for over half an hour. I was about to say something when Harry nudged me.

"This next one might be worth a bid."

I sat up and paid closer attention. The price began to rise steadily; it seemed the bidding was between Harry and a couple of people behind us. I didn't dare turn round in case the auctioneer thought I was putting in a bid. The price went over our agreed maximum, so Harry dropped out.

More cars passed through. I became increasingly glad Harry

had insisted we visit the toilet before the bidding started, otherwise I'm sure I'd have been squirming.

Despite not needing to relieve myself, I gradually became aware that my nose was itching. I wanted to reach up and scratch it, but knew I couldn't. As the bidding continued, the urge became almost impossible to deny. As soon as the auctioneer's gavel buzzer sounded my hand shot up to my right nostril and gave it a good rub.

Mark smiled over at me. He must have noticed the trouble I'd been having.

The next car was another Harry had his eye on. We were still just within the budget, and Harry signalled his bid. No one else raised a hand.

This is the one', I thought. But at the last second another bid was made, and the car slipped out of our hands.

"Damn, that was close," Harry said.

"Sorry, but I can't go any higher than what we agreed."

"No problem. It's all part of the fun," Harry smiled, clearly enjoying himself. I knew he did this sort of thing all the time for his friends. That's how I'd known he was the man to take with us.

A few more cars went through. Some didn't reach their reserves and weren't sold. Then another one Harry had highlighted in the auction catalogue came along. It was a six-year-old silver Ford Cortina. Harry said it was a little older than he would have liked, but "is in pretty good nick." What had swayed Harry was the reasonably low mileage.

The bidding began. This time it was between Harry and someone on the front row. Our maximum was coming up. The guy in front signalled a bid, Harry waited a second or two and raised his catalogue. I watched the man in front to see if he would bid again. I waited, and waited, but the next sound I heard was the auctioneer's electronic buzzer.

It took me a moment to realise Harry was the successful bidder. I owned a car! It felt wonderful. I shook Harry's hand, and gave Mark's knee a quick squeeze.

Because of my inaction due to the shock, we had to wait until the next car had been sold before we could leave the seated area and make our way to the counter round the corner where new owners signed all the necessary papers.

"Look, Harry, if you hadn't come with us, goodness knows what I'd have ended up buying. I'm…we're so grateful."

"I'm just keeping in with the boss," Harry smiled.

I'd forgotten I was Harry's boss. "Well, whenever you need your leave chit signing, just bring it to me."

Harry laughed. "I would anyway, you're the only one who can sign off on leave requests."

"You knew what I meant. If ever I can be of help to you at work, let me know."

"Thanks, Simon, I will."

The auctioneers would hold my car for a few days until the cheque cleared. I'd booked in for a couple of refresher driving lessons. Hopefully by the end of the week I would feel confident enough to drive my car home. Harry offered to bring me back to the car auctions on Friday so I wouldn't have to take the bus.

THE WEEK WENT by quickly; I was coming to terms with the new job; it was very different from my old post. The biggest downside was not interacting with the public as much. I'd thought of a few good ideas to help liven things up—I'd mentioned these in my interview—and they seemed to be well received.

I wanted to hire a children's storyteller. The budget wouldn't stretch to paying them much, this was local government after all. However, if I was able to find the right person, he or she would come in a few lunchtimes a week. They'd either read a story from a book, or better still, improvise. Puppets or some other props would certainly keep the little ones entertained. As it was programmed for the middle of the day, the stories would have to be aimed at the pre-schoolers. At least during term time. I typed up my proposal and submitted it to the town hall. There would have to be costings, logistics reports, and goodness knows how many other things to sign and stamp before any action would be taken.

I couldn't believe it when I received a memo that said that due to the spiralling cost of ballpoint pens, in future all new pens would have to be signed for before being issued. I scrunched up the memo and filed it in the appropriate receptacle.

THE REFRESHER DRIVING lessons weren't as bad as I'd feared. The instructor, a man in his early fifties, had a warm and friendly manner; I guess this was severely tested by some of his less-able students. I told him I'd passed my test about six years previously, but apart from the few times I'd driven my dad's car, I hadn't been behind the wheel.

As I checked the mirrors and turned on the ignition, everything seemed to fall back into place. I managed to do all the usual things like check mirror, signal, manoeuvre; uphill and downhill starts; in-line parking; and three point turns. I even did fairly well in traffic, something I knew I wasn't confident with.

"Well, young man," the instructor said when I'd parked the dual-control car outside my house. "I'll see you again tomorrow night. I see no reason why you shouldn't finish with that second lesson. You're a good driver, considerate to other road users and you don't take unnecessary risks."

SAM WAS LOOKING out for me as I passed his house on Thursday evening. "Wait up. I've got my bags inside. Can you give me a hand with them?"

Paul was in the kitchen when we entered. "Am I glad to see you! This one has been looking out of the window every couple of minutes for the past half hour."

"Daaaad!"

I laughed. "You could have gone over earlier. Mark should be home."

"I'd forgotten that, sorry."

"It's probably your dad you should be apologising to for driving him up the wall."

"He was okay. It's great to see him so excited. I doubt if he'll even miss us."

"Of course I'll miss you," he said, "I'll even miss Charlotte… well, a bit anyway."

Reaching into his pocket and pulling out his wallet, Paul said, "I know it isn't cheap to feed this bottomless pit." He held out a twenty pound note.

"I don't want anything." I shook my head. "And that's far too much."

"Use it to take him out if you want."

Reluctantly I took the money.

Helen entered the kitchen. "Thanks for agreeing to look after Sam. I wouldn't have liked him to miss school, which he would have had to do if we'd taken him with us."

"No problem. So you two go away, have a great time and relax."

"JUST THINK," I said to the others as we were walking back from the supermarket, "this will be the last time we have to carry our groceries all the way home."

"It's surprising how much everything weighs," Mark said.

"When do you collect the car?" Sam asked.

"Tomorrow after work. Do you want to come with us?"

"Wow, can I?"

"Sure," Mark said. "But we'll have to wait until about seven o'clock because Simon doesn't want to drive in rush hour traffic till he's gotten used to driving again."

We explained to Sam that it had been a while since I last drove.

"Does the car have a sun roof and everything?"

"Good grief, no. We couldn't afford anything as fancy as that."

"Do you think we'll be able to go out somewhere at the weekend?" Sam asked.

"Can't see why not. We could drive into the country, go for a walk, and find somewhere to have a meal on the way home. How does that sound to everyone?"

Two voices were raised in assent.

MY CHIEF GOAL on Friday was to leave as soon as knocking off time arrived, so I could go for my car. The clock dragged its way through the day at a snail's pace.

Every niggling problem, everything that seemingly could go wrong, did, including the fire alarm going off. This necessitated the evacuation of the building. The fire brigade had to come out and investigate. It turned out to be a faulty sensor.

Finally it was four-thirty; we closed half an hour earlier on Fridays. I had to check that all the other librarians had signed out, then I left the building in the care of the cleaners.

After eating dinner with Mark and Sam, I started clock-watching again.

Harry showed up a little early and drove Mark, Sam, and myself to the auction rooms.

Once the last bit of paperwork was completed, Harry left and Mark, Sam and I walked to where the Ford was waiting. Mark and Sam tossed a coin to see who would sit in the front passenger's seat. Mark won, but—bless his heart—he let Sam ride up front anyway. It occured to me that perhaps Mark thought it would be safer in the back. I'd have to ask him about that.

Apart from a woman stepping out in front of me when we were driving down a side street, the journey home was uneventful. My unfamiliarity with the layout of the car's controls meant I squirted the windscreen instead of sounding the horn at the wayward pedestrian. I knew neither Mark nor Sam would let me live that one down.

WE GOT UP early the next day to allow ourselves plenty of time for our day trip. We'd decided the night before to visit Haworth and the parsonage where the Bronte sisters had lived. I was certain the Brontes would come up in set texts for Sam, so I thought it would help him to get to see where many of the famous novels had been written.

I'd studied the road maps the previous night and was confident I could get there with little difficulty.

We pulled in at a car park about half-past ten. After visiting the loo, we decided to stretch our legs. Passing a bookshop, I just had to go in, much to Mark and Sam's amusement.

"See, I only bought this," I said, emerging ten minutes later waving a guidebook, one thin enough to qualify as a booklet.

"Yeah, but I saw you stopping to stroke that leather-bound set of Charlotte Bronte novels," Sam said.

Mark sniggered. I shot him a look before opening my guidebook.

"Says here there's a walk which takes us past the Stanbury Reservoir, the Bronte Falls, the Bronte Bridge, and the Bronte Stone Chair."

"They make a lot of the Bronte sisters don't they?" Sam observed.

"What's the Bronte chair?" Mark asked.

I read from the guidebook. "The stone chair is where the sisters took turns to sit and write their first stories." I looked up from the book. "Want to do that walk?"

AFTER LUNCH—SANDWICHES and soft drinks that we'd brought with us—we decided to visit the Parsonage.

I was disappointed with the interior of the building. Most things were behind glass cases. The large number of people in the place didn't help either. Sam was surprised at the smallness of the dresses and bonnets the sisters had worn, so he at least got something useful from the visit.

"IT'S SO BLEAK out here," Mark said.

We'd decided to go for another walk on the moors.

I turned around and regarded our surroundings. "It brings alive the images I got when I read Wuthering Heights," I said.

"I never read that one," Mark confessed.

"I'll dig out my copy sometime."

We'd promised Sam a ride on the restored Keighley and Worth Valley steam railway.

"Did either of you see the film *The Railway Children*?" I asked.

"Yeah, years ago," Mark said.

"It was filmed here."

AFTER GETTING OFF the train, I looked up at the sky; storm clouds were beginning to gather, so we decided to head home. As promised, we stopped off at a country pub for dinner. We were caught in the storm, but the car and my nerves managed really well.

BACK AT HOME Mark and I stretched out on the couch while Sam got himself comfortable in the armchair.

"Thanks for taking us out," Sam said. "It's so different seeing stuff for real rather than just reading about it in books."

"Yeah, thanks, love." Mark pulled me to him and gave me a kiss.

I snuggled against his chest. "My pleasure." I yawned. "It's a lot easier getting to places by car."

We sat for a while just gazing into the fire, warming our toes.

"Do you want to watch anything on the telly, Sam?" Mark asked.

"No thanks. But put on some music if you want."

"I've got a new Country and Western tape."

Both Sam and I groaned.

I could feel the laughter in Mark's chest.

"Or, there's the tape I got of the movie soundtrack to South Pacific." Mark went on to tell Sam that it was the first film that he and I had watched together.

Sam shrugged. "I'll probably just fall asleep right here," he said, closing his eyes and shuffling lower in the chair.

I didn't know about Mark, but as the music played softly in the background it brought back both happy and sad memories. Happy, in that it reminded me of the time we cuddled together watching the film, and sad because of the circumstances that Mark was in at that time. I took his hand at one point, and gave it a squeeze. He squeezed it back.

WE'D BOUGHT A loaf of thick sliced bread at the supermarket, and as the fire had settled down to a steady glow, I asked the pair if they wanted some fire toast.

Sam's house didn't have a real fire, so he wasn't sure if he'd like it.

"Tell you what," Mark said, "I'll do a slice for you, and if you don't like it I'll eat it myself."

Sam agreed.

Mark skewered the first slice on the toasting fork and held

it near the glowing coals. Once it had been toasted to his satisfaction, he took the bread off the fork, turned the slice over, and toasted the other side. Whilst it was still warm he spread it with butter, put it on a plate and handed it to Sam. The teen gave the toast a cautious sniff, then took a tentative bite. The butter started running down his chin.

"Here." I handed him a piece of paper towel.

"It's great!" Sam said stuffing more into his mouth. "Sorry." He chewed rapidly, then swallowed. "But it really is good."

I shook my head and told him there was still a spot of melted butter on his chin.

IN BED THAT evening—me spooned behind Mark as usual—I finally raised something that had been on my mind. "It was kind of you to let Sam have the front seat when we drove home from the car auction yesterday. You weren't frightened of my driving, were you?"

Mark laughed. "No, love, honest. I just thought he'd like to ride in front."

I kissed the back of his head, content with his answer. "Goodnight my angel."

Chapter 6

NO SMELL OF frying bacon or brewing coffee greeted us on Sunday morning. However, once we were all downstairs, Sam offered to make breakfast, but I told him I didn't expect him to cook for us every weekend.

I poured bowls of cereal, which I followed up with scrambled eggs, sausages, and some tomatoes that were only fit for frying. Not the healthiest of breakfasts, but it was Sunday.

We sent Sam to the newsagent's for the Sunday papers and then Mark and I sat on the sofa reading while Sam did a last bit of homework. I had to smile, because when I'd been his age I'd often left homework until the last minute.

After an hour or so catching up on the gossip and scandal of the rich and famous—which most papers seemed to thrive on—we decided to go for a walk. This time we chose the park. I'd spent many happy hours there when I was younger. I'd often volunteered to take next door's dog with me. We didn't have a dog ourselves as mum is allergic to pet hair. I'd had to be careful to brush myself down if the dog had been moulting.

We approached the swings, and, as no one was watching, all three of us got on.

We spent an enjoyable time just fooling around, laughing, and gently teasing each other.

"This is great," Mark said after coming down the slide.

"I think it does us good to regress to childhood now and again."

A pained expression swept across Mark's face.

"I'm sorry, my angel, I know you want to forget some of your childhood."

"I'm okay. I remember Mum would bring me to the park sometimes when I was little. It's one of my fondest memories of her."

"We don't have to come here again if it's too painful."

Mark shook his head. "Parks bring back happy memories, and I want to remember those times."

I gave him a hug and was surprised when Sam joined in as well.

The weather was unseasonably bright and warm, so when we got to the pub we decided to sit outside in the beer garden. A few of the tubs had some early flowers out, but it wouldn't be until June before the main blooms showed themselves.

"I like it out here," Mark said when I returned with our drinks.

"Yeah, it's even better in the summer." I grew quiet as happy memories floated through my mind. "I remember once my dad sneaked me out a couple of half pints of dry cider. I felt absolutely fine. Don't think my speech was slurred or anything. But when I stood up I immediately fell over."

The others laughed.

"I thought you said the first time you got drunk was when

you were at your Gran's?" Mark asked.

"I don't count the cider incident as getting drunk. As I said, I could talk and think properly. It was just my legs wouldn't co-operate with the rest of my body."

Sam continued to laugh.

"No, the time with Gran didn't happen here. I was staying with her for the weekend. She had a house just over the way there." I pointed with my glass to my right. "Her next door neighbour, Miss Finch, was renowned for her homemade wine. Many's the tradesman who was invited in 'Just for a small glass of my latest creation.' And found himself a little the worse for wear soon afterwards."

Sam's eyes widened.

"Miss Finch's niece had been strawberry picking and Miss Finch—she was always Miss Finch to me, never Maggie—had turned the fruit she couldn't eat into wine. I swear that woman can make wine out of anything.

"So," I took a pull on my pint, "she'd brewed up the strawberries and they were all in little bottles in her kitchen. She'd no doubt run out of standard wine bottles. I thought they looked like cherryade, and asked her if I could have a bottle. She probably thought I was going to give it to Gran."

"Oh no," Sam said.

"I went into the field behind their houses and drank the entire bottle. Was I sick! I was still poorly the next day when Mum came to collect me. Gran just told her what had happened. Mum hit the roof. Mind you I didn't touch another drop for years after that."

The others were in stitches with my tale of woe. Even Mark, who didn't like stories about getting drunk, found it funny.

"At least you learnt your lesson," Mark said.

I nodded. "Two pints is my limit."

"Good," was his only reaction.

I squeezed Mark's knee. He smiled back at me.

❖

THE THREE OF us were relaxing in the living room when the phone rang. It was Paul and Helen. International calls were very expensive back in the mid 1980's, so I told Sam not to be on for long. Mark and I went into the kitchen to give him some privacy.

When the call ended, Sam joined us in the kitchen. I could tell from his face he was glad to have heard from them.

"Have you missed them, mate?" Mark asked.

He nodded. "They said the weather was really hot out there. Dad's getting a tan. Mum prefers to sit in the shade with Charlotte."

THE NEXT WEEK at work passed quickly. Permission came down from on high to seek the services of a storyteller. I had a couple of suitable candidates in mind so set about contacting them to see if they were interested. My favoured candidate wasn't in. I decided to hold off on calling the other for the moment.

It was great to come home at the end of each day to find the two men in my life waiting for me. Mark, Sam, and I were rapidly forming a close family bond.

On Friday night I asked the two of them if they fancied a visit to the fair. It had set up on the Common just out of town a day or so earlier. Needless to say they were both enthusiastic about the idea. So after grabbing a quick meal, we piled into the car and set off.

The fairground's car park was almost filled to capacity, but luckily someone was just pulling out so I managed to get a space not too far from the entrance. As we drew closer to the fair itself we were beset by the familiar food smells of fried onions, hotdogs, toffee apples, and candy floss. These all mixed disagreeably with the smell of diesel fumes from the many generators, damp earth, and fermented mown grass.

None of the rides we went on was particularly scary; but the little dipper and the octopus were the closest the fair came to offering something that could be called 'white knuckle.'

Sam spotted the Dodgems. "Can we go on those?"

Each car held two people, so Mark and I took it in turns to drive Sam around the little arena while the other had a car to himself. We must have spent half an hour bumping into each other plus anyone else in range.

"Okay, you two," I said. "I think it's time we got something to eat."

Mark and I had a hot dog, Sam chose a hamburger. We walked around the rest of the fair eating our junk food. I got a couple of pounds changed into 2 pence pieces, and we spent a while on the slot machines. Some of the machines took 10p each time, had loads of flashing lights, nudge buttons and the rest, but we decided the old-fashioned one armed bandits with the pull-down levers were the best. As they only took 2p a time, we felt we got more for our money. Sam and I were Yorkshiremen and I classed Mark as an honorary one, too. And as I told Mark, Yorkshire folk are "careful with their brass."

Mark had a go on the rifle range and scored a few bulls eyes. When the man asked him what prize he wanted, he chose a little brown teddy bear with a red ribbon tied round his neck. As soon as he'd stepped away from the booth, Mark gave the bear to me. I wanted to kiss him so badly, but there were too many people about. I had to content myself with a whispered "I love you," and a squeeze to Mark's elbow.

"He'll keep Humphrey company," Mark said before returning the squeeze to my elbow.

Next on the agenda was the Ghost Train. Each car had four seats but we managed to get a car to ourselves. I sat in the back with Mark and Sam in the front. I can't really describe this ride, as I spent the whole time with my eyes shut and my fingers in my ears.

"Wimp!" Sam said when the ride had come to a halt.

To deflect attention from myself I asked Sam if he wanted to go on the Ferris wheel next.

He did.

"Hi, Sam," said a stocky, brown-haired boy in jeans, black T-shirt, and jean jacket. "I wondered if I'd see you here."

"Hi, Billy. I'm here with a couple of my neighbours. Simon and Mark." He pointed to us.

"Hello," Billy said to us.

We returned his greeting.

"Have you come with your mum and dad?" Sam asked Billy.

"No, my uncle Bill brought me. He's just gone to the loo."

"We were just going to go on the Ferris wheel," Sam looked over at the large brightly lit wheel.

"We've been on that, you can see for miles when you're at the top," Billy told us.

At this point a man who must have been in his mid-thirties came along and put a hand on Billy's shoulder.

"Uncle Bill, this is Sam, he's in my class at school."

Bill frowned, then his face cleared. "Billy's mentioned you. Nice to see you at last."

"Hello, Mr erm…"

"Call me Bill."

"Thanks. My neighbours brought me to the fair, mum and dad are on holiday with my baby sister. I'm staying with them for a while."

Bill's frown returned. "Right, I was just going to take Billy on the Dodgems."

"Err, yeah," Sam said, trying to ignore the hostility Bill was displaying. "We've been on those, They're great!"

"We'll probably see you later on then," Billy said as his uncle guided him away.

"Wonder what his problem was?" Mark asked me when Bill and Billy had gone.

"Probably worked out our relationship." Though how he could, I didn't know.

Mark shrugged.

Billy was right, the view from the top of the Ferris wheel was good and the lights of the town spread out below us spread out to the horizon.

"IS BILLY A close friend?" I asked Sam on the way home.

Sam didn't reply.

"Anything wrong, mate?" Mark asked him.

"I wish he was my boyfriend."

I didn't know what to say, and judging by the silence, Mark didn't either.

Finally Mark said, "Do you know if he feels the same way about you?"

"I'm not sure," Sam said quietly.

"Has he ever mentioned that he has a girlfriend?"

"No."

"Has he ever said anything bad about gays?" Mark asked.

"It's never come up."

"It isn't easy to bring any conversation around to being gay," I put in.

"True," Mark said.

"Could you talk about your family, then say that you wish you saw more of your uncle Steve, and bring up his sexuality somehow?" It wasn't a very satisfactory way of bringing up the subject, but I had little experience of teenage matchmaking. I was always too terrified to approach anyone when I was Sam's age.

"That might work," Sam said.

"Do it on neutral territory," Mark suggested. "I'm not sure, but I think his uncle Bill might suspect something of Billy's feelings. He gave Simon and me a hard look earlier when you said you were staying with us. So if you do want to talk about this with Billy, make sure his uncle isn't around."

"I will. Thanks."

"But please be careful. Coming out to friends is a brave thing to do. Although the rewards might be great, the possible consequences could be just as heavy," I warned.

"Simon's right," Mark put in. "It's easy to misunderstand a friend's interest, thinking…hoping it's more than it is. Many gay men have missed the signals and…well, gotten hurt."

Sam stayed quiet for the rest of the drive home.

WE DECIDED TO take a trip to Scarborough on Saturday. I pointed out it wasn't exactly high season, so many of the seaside attractions wouldn't be open. However, with no other reasonable suggestions put forward, I pointed the Ford coastward.

There was little difficulty in finding a parking spot, as there were few tourists at that time of year. However, the sun was doing its best to warm us up. We walked along the seafront. Despite prompting from Sam, no way was I going to roll up my trousers and go for a paddle at the water's edge.

"I like my feet the colour they are," I told him, "Not black with frostbite."

During our walk we spotted a seafood stand open for business. I don't like many shellfish, but give me a tub of peeled prawns with some vinegar on them, and I'm happy. Sam and Mark plumped for a bag of whelks. They offered me one. The thought of putting something chewy and fishy in my mouth caused my stomach to rebel, so I declined their kind offer.

Sam spotted an amusement arcade.

"Didn't you have enough of the one-armed bandits yesterday?" Mark asked him.

Sam shook his head. "I love playing the slot machines," he countered.

"Here's a couple of quid." Mark handed him two one-pound coins. "See how long you can make them last. Simon and me'll be in the café next door. Okay?"

"Thanks," Sam said before heading towards the bright flashing lights of the arcade.

"I hope Paul and Helen don't think we've turned their son into a gambler," I said to Mark as we sat at a table with coffee and sticky buns.

"He'll be okay. I used to play the slot machines when I was his age, and I survived."

I reached for his hand under the table. Mark had survived much worse and come out the other side sweet, kind and gentle.

A while later Sam came into the café.

"Spent up already, mate?" Mark asked him.

"Yeah, the machines weren't as good as those at the fair yesterday. Can I have a Coke?"

"And what's the magic word?" Was I doing my old fuddy-duddy thing again, or trying to be a good pseudo-parent by teaching Sam good manners?

"Sorry. May I have a Coke, please."

I was glad he'd corrected his grammar, too, I wouldn't have pulled him up for that though. I fished out some money, and Sam went to the counter to order his drink.

After we'd finished eating and drinking, I said, "Right, who's for a look round the shops, and then find a nice fish and chip restaurant?"

"FANCY SEEING YOU here!" a voice said as its owner put his hand on my shoulder.

I turned round to find Terry, the man whose job I was now doing at the library. "Hi Terry. Yeah, we were at a loose end, and we've got Sam, a neighbour, to look after for a couple of weeks, so we thought we'd check out the coast."

"How did you get here? I didn't think there were any trains between Littleborough and Scarborough this time of year."

"Simon bought a car, so we're now mobile," Mark put in.

"About time," Terry smiled.

"Lack of funds," I shrugged. "Now I've got the promotion, things are a bit easier."

"How's it going, the job I mean?" Terry asked.

"Fine. Different from being a librarian in a department, though."

"You'll adjust." Terry smiled. "Got used to all the paper shuffling yet?"

I groaned. "I doubt I ever will. I can't see the need for half of it."

Terry laughed. "You're telling me. I'm glad I'm out of it."

"Are you and…Mabel enjoying retirement?" I asked, remembering Terry's wife's name at the last second.

"He smiled. "It's great not having to get up early in the morning, and knowing that you don't have to face a day at work."

"Must be," I said. "Well anyway, we were just having a mooch round till we got hungry, then we were going for fish and chips."

Terry told us where the best places to eat were and we promised to check them out.

AFTER LUNCH WE did a bit more sightseeing. Mark wanted to get a stick of rock to take back home for Daphne.

"Keeping in with the boss?" Sam asked.

"Of course. She's got a sweet tooth, and you never know when I might need to cash in my Brownie points."

THE SMELL OF frying bacon wakened me Sunday morning. As Mark was still asleep, Sam had to be making us breakfast. He was a great kid. I hoped that if Billy were gay, he and Sam would make it.

"You didn't have to cook us breakfast, mate," Mark said when we came downstairs.

"I know, but I didn't wake up in time last Sunday, and as this will be the last Sunday we're together, I set my alarm clock to make sure I'd get up."

I didn't want to think about how this would be our last Sunday together.

After breakfast, Mark told Sam to go and watch the telly or something while he and I cleaned up the kitchen. Sam agreed after a token protest.

"As the rain seems to be holding off," I said, looking out of the living room window at a dull but dry street, "do you want to go for a walk and maybe a drink at the pub afterward?" I asked Sam.

"Can we go to the woods?" he asked.

"Can't see why not, mate," Mark said.

So we put on our coats and headed out. Once the trees provided us with sufficient screening, Mark took my right hand in his left. I could never tire of this simple act of affection. I gave him a peck on the cheek.

Sam spotted this and smiled. "I hope I find a boyfriend soon."

"A lovely lad like you shouldn't have too much trouble finding the right boy. Just be careful," I said.

"Thanks. I hope it'll be Billy. We just get on so well together."

"Who knows, he might feel the same way about you. But like I said, you need to be careful."

"I know, thanks."

We chased each other through the trees. The ground was too damp to wrestle, so we just played tag. I was out of breath by the time we got to the pub.

AFTER PUTTING THE Sunday roast in the oven and preparing the potatoes and vegetables for later cooking, I went back into the living room and sat next to Mark on the sofa.

"It's great living here," Sam said from the easy chair. "I love Mum and Dad, but with you two, well, it's different, you know?"

"We understand," Mark said.

"I can be myself here. I know mum and dad are okay with me being gay, but…they can't know what it's like."

"Yeah," Mark said.

"You're welcome to stay here whenever you want. We love having you. You're the nearest thing that Mark and I will ever have to a son of our own."

"I hadn't thought of it like that. I've got my real dad of course, but it would be cool to have a couple of, well, honorary dads, too."

I looked over at Mark. He, like me, was trying to blink back tears.

"That's the nicest thing you've ever said to us. We'd be really chuffed to be your honorary dads," Mark sniffed.

Both Mark and I stood and approached Sam's chair to give our son a hug.

"YOU KNOW," MARK said, seating himself at the kitchen table, "Before I came to Yorkshire I had no idea Yorkshire pudding was served as a separate course by itself. At home whenever mum made Yorkshire pudding it was just put on the plate with the rest of the dinner."

"Really?" Sam said. Like me he was used to eating the pudding separately.

"I think the reason for it being served first was the pudding was a fairly cheap foodstuff, and you would satisfy your hunger on that so you wouldn't need to eat as much of the more expensive main course," I said, taking two Yorkshire pudding tins—each containing four puddings—out of the oven and bringing them to the table.

"Typical Yorkshire folk, being careful with their brass,"

Mark grinned, taking three puddings from one of the tins.

I LOOKED OUT of the living room window after dinner and saw that the long-threatened rain had arrived.

Sam suggested putting in a video.

After some negotiation, Mark and I got our way and I started *Brief Encounter.*

"What is it about watching old films on a rainy Sunday afternoon?" Mark asked, snuggling up to me on the sofa.

I was about to reply that they held a great deal more appeal now I had someone to watch them with, when…

"Black and white!" Sam said with mock disgust. "How old are you two anyway? Maybe I should call you both Granddad rather than Dad."

Mark threw a cushion at him. "Shut up and watch or go upstairs and do your homework."

"Already done it." Sam grinned, threw the cushion back, and turned his attention back to the screen.

I laid my head on Mark's chest and he put his arm around me. Sighing, I settled down to watch Trevor Howard and Celia Johnson do their thing. I knew the film was remade years later, and was a disaster. *Brief Encounter* is one of those films that didn't work in Technicolor.

My eyes were growing heavy. The glowing coals in the fire making the room cosy and warm, snuggling up with my boyfriend, something romantic playing on the telly…

"Simon?" Mark shook me.

"Err, what's happening?" I sat up and rubbed my eyes.

"You were snoring, love," Mark said.

Sam giggled. "Thought someone was using a chainsaw on the tree outside."

I threw the much-travelled cushion at Sam, looked at the blank TV screen and asked, "Has the film finished?"

"Yeah, she went back to her boring husband." Sam threw the cushion back at me.

"I know, I've seen the film loads of times."

"Yeah, I know, I was just teasing," Sam said. "Is it all right if I have a can of Coke?"

I nodded.

"Do you two want a cup of coffee?"

"Please." I yawned.

While Sam was making the coffee I used the time alone to show Mark just how much I loved him.

Sam coughed. I looked up from atop Mark and gave Sam a sheepish smile. Sam grinned and set the two mugs he was carrying on the TV dining table he'd also brought out.

"So," Mark said once he and I had rearranged ourselves, "what do you want to do now, Sam? The weather hasn't improved."

I looked out the window at a now dark and very dismal scene. The streetlights were being reflected in puddles of rainwater.

"Have you got any board games?" Sam asked.

"Have a look in that drawer." I pointed to the video shelves. I'd kept the games that I'd played as a child. Apart from the peg solitaire, which I was able to solve all too quickly, the rest of the games hadn't been touched in years.

Sam pulled out the box of Monopoly. "Can we play this?"

"Mark?" I looked over at my boyfriend.

Mark shrugged. "Haven't played Monopoly in years."

Sam managed to snatch up the more desirable properties early on, and once he was able to build hotels on them, it was only a matter of time before he cleaned us out.

Mark and I exacted our revenge by tackling Sam to the carpet and tickling him until he said he was sorry.

Mark sat across Sam's chest. "Now you'll let me win next time, won't you?"

"Of course."

Mark rolled off Sam.

"In your dreams," Sam yelled, running across the room. This brought on another attack from us.

All three of us eventually collapsed, winded, on the sofa, in a tangled mass of arms and legs.

Chapter 7

FOR ONCE, MONDAY was a good day at work. I'd managed to persuade Miss Finch, Gran's ex-neighbour and wine-maker extraordinaire, to be the storyteller for the children's section. She'd never married, and as she didn't have any grandchildren to spoil, she relished the opportunity to fulfill the grandmotherly role. I well remember her stories when I was little. I spent most of my weekends with Gran, and I'd often nip next door to see Miss Finch. She'd sit me down, give me one of her home-made biscuits and a bottle of pop; I only sampled her wine that one time. She'd then tell me about life in 'the olden days'. I was never sure how true these stories were, but I would sit there for hours, enraptured by her words. She not only had a good command of language, she told her stories in interesting ways, too.

She often became really animated during these sessions. I knew the children in the library would love her stories. Not to mention the biscuits. Best of all, as far as the local authority was concerned, she didn't want any payment for her time, either.

It was a happy senior librarian who unlocked his front door that evening. "Hi, honey, I'm home! Got a kiss for your boyfriend?"

I came to a sudden halt. Framed in the kitchen door were Sam and his friend Billy. I felt my face heat, and it had nothing to do with the fire blazing in the grate.

"Hi, Mr Peters," Billy said.

"Uh, hi."

"Sam invited me round for a bit, I hope you don't mind?" Billy said, his face turning red also, though it was nothing to the glow I suspected I was sporting.

"Erm, no, Billy. You're very welcome. Is Mark around?"

Mark was in the kitchen, trying none too successfully to keep a straight face. "Simon, you are…were in a good mood?"

"Yeah, I had a good day at work."

Conversation was awkward. Sam eventually asked Billy if he wanted to go and see the room where he was staying. The two of them quickly left the scene.

"Oh shit!" I said once they were out of earshot.

Mark couldn't hold it in any longer. "I wish I had seen your face when you noticed Billy. I bet it was a picture."

"Yeah. I guess I've just outed us."

Mark laughed. "Yep, love, you certainly did."

"Jesus, how embarrassing."

"Never mind," Mark said, wrapping his arms around me. "Want a drink? You look like you need one."

"I could, but I'll stick to coffee."

Mark started messing with the coffee maker. "So, what put you in such a good mood?"

I told him about Miss Finch.

"So long as she doesn't get them drunk on her homemade

wine," Mark said.

I smiled and told Mark I seriously doubted she'd bring any wine with her. "It was only my own sneakiness that got me a taste that one time. She never to my knowledge gave the stuff to kids."

"That's a relief. I'd hate an angry parent kicking up a stink because their little darling came home legless from the library," Mark laughed.

We then heard the thundering of two pairs of teenage feet racing down the stairs.

"Mark, Simon!" Sam came into the room holding Billy's hand. "Billy's agreed we can be boyfriends…" Sam continued to gabble while still holding onto a blushing Billy.

It seemed that while they were upstairs, Billy had asked Sam if Mark and I were partners. Sam couldn't deny the obvious. Billy had then confessed he was envious. Realising what he'd said Billy had tried to run off, but Sam had caught him and kissed him.

"Billy said he's had a crush on me for ages." Sam blushed.

"That's a relief because Sam's been gaga over you for weeks, too," Mark said.

Billy laughed, and Sam stuck his tongue out at Mark.

Just then the coffee maker finished doing its thing and I asked everyone if they wanted a cup. As usual Sam asked for tea instead.

After setting the mugs on the table, I asked Billy, "Sam's mum and dad know about him being gay, do your parents know about you?"

Billy's face, that until then had been the picture of radiance, turned pensive. I regretted asking the question.

"No, they don't. My uncle Bill guessed though. He caught me checking another boy out once. He wasn't too pleased but he promised not to say anything to Mum and Dad. I don't know what they'll say when I tell them."

"You can see each other at Sam's place or here." Mark looked over at me for agreement.

I nodded.

"So you'll be okay until you're ready to come out more fully. Don't rush it. Only tell them when you're ready."

Billy nodded. "Thanks. I don't think I'll be able to tell them for a while yet."

"Like Mark said, don't rush it." I got up to start serving the meal Mark had prepared. "Can you stay and eat with us?" I asked Billy.

"Please, Billy," Sam implored.

At first Billy looked uncertain, then slowly a smile broke across his face. "Yeah, okay, thanks."

I told Billy to telephone his parents to tell them where he was and to get permission to stay.

It was cute watching Sam and Billy so happy. Sam decided he would feed Billy, no doubt remembering when I had to do the same for Mark. Billy tried to repeat the favour for Sam, but the whole thing soon descended into uncontrollable laughter as food went everywhere.

LATER, WHEN BILLY had gone home, and Sam had decided to have an early night, I put on some light classical music with the volume turned down.

"Isn't young love grand?" I asked, rejoining Mark on the settee.

"Billy and Sam?"

I nodded.

Pulling me toward him, Mark said, "Were we that bad when we finally found each other?"

"Worse. I couldn't believe that such a handsome hunk said he loved me. I kept having to pinch myself." I nuzzled Mark's neck.

"Silly," Mark chuckled. "I'll never forget that Christmas Day."

"The day I got the best gift ever."

"Me, too." Mark started undoing my belt. "At least it'll be

easy to remember our anniversary."

"Stop it." I slapped at Mark's hand had just gotten hold of a certain rather firm part of my anatomy through my trousers. "Sam could come down and see us."

"So? It's not like he doesn't have one of his own." Mark gave my dick a squeeze. "But not one as nice as this." He started to pull down my zip.

"Mark!" Then realising I was talking too loudly, I said, "We can't."

Mark pouted. "I wouldn't care, we didn't have the fun of creating him, but we've got to suffer the pains of having him."

I thumped his arm. "You don't mean that."

Mark's expression softened. "Nope, 'course I don't." He kissed me.

As we continued to argue good-naturedly I noticed two things. Mark hadn't removed his hand and my dick hadn't softened.

"Want to take this to the bedroom?" I asked, knowing that at least there was a lock on the bedroom door.

"So long as he's coming, too." Mark gave my dick another squeeze.

"Oh, I think he'll be coming." I laughed.

"ONE QUESTION HAS been answered tonight," I said after Mark and I had made love and the lights had been turned out.

"That I'm the sexiest man in Littleborough?" Mark asked.

I kissed him. "No, silly, that question was answered months ago. And I think you're the sexiest man in the whole of Yorkshire."

"Wow, that's some compliment. I know how some Yorkshiremen think their county is all there is."

"Yeah, right." Though I knew he wasn't exaggerating too much. Yorkshire folk tended to be rather proud of their county of birth.

"I suppose I'll have to watch you if we ever go outside the

county boundaries."

"Like I just said, yeah, right."

We fooled around a bit more until Mark reminded me of my original point.

"It's your fault, you're such a distraction."

"Thanks." Mark kissed me. "But your point?"

"You expect me to concentrate when you're kissing me?" I murmured close to his lips.

"Simon! That's it, I'm cutting you off until you tell me what first started this." Mark retreated to his side of the bed.

I harrumphed. "Okay. We know the answer to the question of why Billy's uncle gave us that nasty look. He must have twigged that Billy liked Sam, and with Sam saying that he was staying with us, I guess the bigot put two and two together."

"And came up with something unpleasant, at least in his mind."

"Exactly."

"I hope Bill keeps his promise, and doesn't spill the beans to Billy's parents," Mark said, leaning over and kissing me again.

"Good to have you back. I missed you." It was my turn to pout, but as it was dark, I doubted Mark could see.

THE REST OF the week passed uneventfully at work—just the usual round of paper shuffling, decision making and settling of minor disputes between colleagues—nothing too exacting.

However, Sam's week had a little more excitement in it. We saw rather a lot of Billy. Not that either Mark or I had any complaints. Billy was a good kid. He soaked up the affection Sam gave him, and wasn't shy about giving affection back. I was pleased the pair felt comfortable enough to display their feelings for each other in front of Mark and me.

When Billy wasn't at our place, Sam was on the phone to him. They'd decided not to meet at Billy's house too often since

Billy didn't want to arouse too much suspicion from his parents.

THURSDAY FOUND THE three of us doing the weekly shopping again. I paused by the wine shelves. After looking at the labels and, yes, the prices, I put a bottle in the trolley.

"Bit pricey isn't it?" Mark asked, nodding at the bottle.

"Tonight's the last night Sam will be with us. So I thought we'd push the boat out. I don't think Paul will mind Sam having a glass with his dinner."

"Could I? That'd be great," Sam beamed.

"Just the one glass."

"Okay." His smile dimmed only slightly.

"How do you fancy the Chinese banquet from The Oriental?" I asked.

Sam's eyes widened. "We only have that at home on really special occasions."

"Can't think of a more special occasion than saying good-bye to our surrogate son," Mark said, resting a hand on Sam's shoulder.

"I'll miss you two," Sam said.

"Not half as much as we'll miss you," I said. "Though it's not as if we'll never see each other again, you only live a couple of doors down."

"I know, but thanks for making my last night special." Sam got a glint in his eye. "But look on the bright side, from tomorrow night you'll be able to chase each other around the house naked."

My mouth fell open and Mark laughed.

"Sam!" I said, looking around to see if anyone was close enough to have overheard. As no one was giving us weird looks, I guessed we'd been lucky.

"Sorry." Sam had the good grace to look abashed, but then spoiled the effect by giggling.

❖

"THIS IS GREAT," Mark said through a mouthful of fried seaweed.

Sam agreed. "Though you'll need to drink lots of water, that stuff's really salty."

"Perhaps we should have only got the meal for two people," I worried, ever the Yorkshireman. "I can't see us getting through all this lot." I waved my hand over a frighteningly large number of foil boxes.

"Don't worry, we'll finish it," Mark said.

"Mum and Dad usually order a bit less than we think we'll need when we get this." Sam had moved on to the spring rolls.

"YOU WERE RIGHT, love," Mark said, lowering himself gingerly onto the couch. "We did order too much."

I laughed.

"I vote for just vegging out in front of the telly for the rest of the evening." Mark rubbed his distended belly.

"Yeah. I can't move much further than the chair," Sam said, crawling over to it.

I too had eaten quite a bit, though not as much as my dining companions. I thought about clearing away the dirty plates, but the couch and Mark's waiting arms were too inviting.

"WELL, I HATE to break up this cosy scene, but we've all got things to do tomorrow." I got to my feet when the headlines on *News At Ten* had been announced.

"True." Mark stood, stretched, and reached for the plates and empty foil boxes on the TV tray tables.

"No, it's okay, angel, I'll do that."

"S'okay." Mark gathered the stuff together and took it into

the kitchen.

Turning to Sam, who was half-dozing in the chair, I shook his shoulder and said, "It's been great having you. Remember, you're welcome here any time, and that goes for Billy, too."

"Thanks." Sam stood and gave me a hug.

ANTICIPATION OF THE weekend usually made for a pleasant Friday at work. However, I knew the upcoming weekend wouldn't be as enjoyable as previous ones because Sam wouldn't be with us. I was sitting brooding about this when Mary breezed into my office.

"Thank God it's Friday!" she said, sitting in my guest chair and kicking off her shoes.

"Hello, stranger." I tried for a smile.

"We haven't seen much of each other lately."

"The price of promotion." I shrugged. "My old post should be filled soon. Then all the work won't fall on your shoulders."

We'd appointed a temp in to cover my old position, and he had applied for the permanent post.

"John's a good lad, and he's got a cute bum."

"Mary!"

"He has. Not as nice as yours, though."

"Thanks, I think."

Getting serious, she said, "I miss working with you. We used to have a good laugh."

I smiled. "You're right, we did."

"It's about missing you that I've popped in. How do you and Mark fancy coming out with Jerry and me tomorrow night?"

"Does he know about, you know, Mark and me?"

"I told him I had a good friend who was gay, but I didn't give him any details. He didn't say anything either way."

"I'd feel happier if you sounded Jerry out first. I don't want any unpleasantness." Even though this was the late 1980s and things had improved a lot, some people still had a hard time accepting same-sex couples.

"Okay."

"Though I'm not sure if either Mark or I will feel like going out tomorrow."

"How come?"

I told her about how Mark and I had grown close to Sam over the past couple of weeks and that Paul and Helen were flying home that day. "We're going to miss him."

"Doesn't he live down the street from you?"

I nodded.

"So it's not as if you'll never see him again."

I knew I was overreacting to Sam's departure and admitted as much. Then I went on to tell Mary what Sam had said about how Mark and I would be free to run about the house naked.

She laughed.

Returning to the topic of our proposed double-date, I said, "And you only get to see Jerry at the weekends. I'd have thought you'd want him all to yourself."

"I think we've gotten past the lovesick, needing to hold on to each other at every moment stage. Don't get me wrong, I still go weak at the knees just at the thought of him."

I laughed. Then I began to think about my reaction each time I saw Mark. "I still can't believe Mark's real. I imagine I'm going to wake up any minute and it'll all have been a dream."

"You silly sod."

"I know." I let out a breath and closed my eyes. "As you know I've never been very outgoing. I just hope Mark doesn't get bored with me." Opening my eyes I told Mary about the nightclub we visited in Leeds. "I hated it and eventually I had to leave."

"Mark's totally besotted with you. You've no need to worry on that score. Trust me."

"I know. It's just my old insecurities playing up again."

"I understand." Mary took my hand and gave it a squeeze.

"Thanks." I found a smile from somewhere. "Enough of this maudlin talk." I looked at my watch. "I think it's about time I knocked off for lunch. If you can get John to cover, we'll go and see what's on offer at Daphne's."

"You just want to go and make goo-goo eyes at Mark."

MARY AND I managed to snag our usual table in the window—it helped to be the boyfriend of one of the waiters—so we were able to people watch, though as both of us were taken, the game had lost much of its fun.

Daphne's was busy, so I only managed to get a few words with Mark before I had to head back to the library and a stack of paperwork I was convinced had spawned offspring during my absence.

A COUPLE OF last-minute snags delayed me, so I was a little late getting home.

When I entered, I thought the house was empty. The lights were off, and the fire wasn't lit. I turned on the light and immediately saw Mark on the sofa. As I approached, I could see the sad expression on his face. I knelt and put my arms around him.

"He's gone home," Mark didn't need to explain whom.

"I know. But we knew Paul and Helen were coming back today." I rocked him in my arms.

"I thought we could all have dinner together one last time. But Paul was in his driveway when I got home. He said he'd come over later and pick up Sam's stuff. When Sam got home from school, Paul came and got Sam's bags from upstairs, and they left."

I rubbed his back. "We had a good time together, let's just concentrate on that."

"Yeah." He let out a breath. "I was being silly."

"No, my angel, you weren't. Sam's become very special to us and we'll miss him, but he's back at home where he belongs."

"I know. He said he'd pop over later."

"Uh huh." We heard someone knocking at the front door. "Probably him now." I got up to answer the door.

"Simon," Paul said.

"Hi. Did you have a nice time?" I opened the door wider to let him in.

"Yeah. It did Helen the world of good." Paul came into the room and spotted Mark, who was still on the settee. "Is this a bad time?"

"No." I asked Paul if he wanted a cup of tea or coffee.

"No thanks, I've just had one. I just came round to thank you for having Sam. He's not shut up about Billy and what a good time he's had here." Paul laughed. "I bet you're glad to have the place to yourselves again, eh?"

The expression on Mark's face soon sobered Paul up.

I indicated for Paul to take a seat. He chose the armchair... Sam's armchair. "Do you remember the day Sam was born?"

"Erm, yeah, why?"

"Was it one of the happiest days of your life?"

"God, yes, I was on top of the world. But what has—"

"As a gay couple, Mark and I can't have a son of our own." I put an arm around Mark's shoulder and pulled him closer. I realised this was the first time I'd showed physical affection to Mark in front of Paul. "We'll never be able to have a kid of our own, do all the things you do with Sam and will do with Charlotte."

"Uh, I guess not," Paul said quietly.

"Although we knew we could only have Sam for a short time, we began to think of him as a part of us...a part of our family. We tried not to get too attached but..." I let out a breath.

"But he's a wonderful kid," Mark put in. "And we did get attached."

"I didn't realise," Paul said.

"There's no reason why you should," Mark said soberly.

"I know Sam thinks the world of you two. I didn't know it went both ways."

"Sam said he loves you and Helen very much, but he had begun to think of Mark and me as kind of honorary dads. I hope that doesn't upset you."

"Wow…no it doesn't upset me. Not at all. I guess the fact that Sam being gay means that you three have a connection…a common bond."

"Yeah. But we don't want to tread on your toes. Sam is your son, and that's how it should be, but…" I swallowed, "I hope you realise what a lucky man you are."

It was Paul's turn to swallow. "I've always loved him, but I guess I've taken our relationship for granted. Yes, you're right, I'm lucky to have him and Charlotte, too."

"Don't worry about it," Mark said. "It's something I bet most straight parents never think about, there's no reason why they should."

"I'm sorry if Sam staying here has caused you pain."

Mark shook his head. "We're honoured you let us share him."

"Thanks for looking at it that way. Oh, almost forgot." Paul held out the plastic bag he'd been holding.

Mark took it, looked inside and burst out laughing. "I was only joking, you didn't have to buy us anything." He pulled out a bottle of vodka.

"I know you didn't mean it," Paul said. "It was just a thank you for looking after Sam."

"We don't need thanking," I said, putting the bottle on the carpet in front of the sofa.

"Yeah, sorry, I know that now. Listen…I'll head off home now. If there's anything I can do, well, you know where I am."

We did and we told him so.

LATER THAT EVENING Mark said, “So, as the kid ain’t here, wanna get naked so I can chase you around the place?”

I laughed, but found myself undressing.

Chapter 8

MARK HAD WANGLED Saturday morning off work. "We need to do something about the back yard this weekend," he urged, unlocking the back door and stepping outside.

I wasn't much of a gardener, and I'd pretty much ignored what went on in the garden. I cut the grass, kept the weeds down as much as I could, but that was about it.

"Why don't we pop down the garden centre and get a few ideas?" I suggested, reaching out to touch a particularly straggly-looking rose bush that needed either pruning or digging up. "Ouch!" I pulled back my hand. "The bugger got me."

Mark let out a single bark of laughter before coming to my aid.

"Let's get some advice on what we can plant." Under my breath I added, "That won't bite."

We went back into the kitchen and I ran my finger under the tap.

"Want me to kiss it better?" Mark asked.

"You can give me a kiss anytime."

So he did.

Just then someone knocked at the front door.

Giddy from Mark's kisses, I said, "If that's the Jehovah's Witnesses, tell them we're devil worshipers and we're about to sacrifice a chicken and they're welcome to come help us."

"Daft bugger," Mark said, going to answer the door. "Sam! How come you knocked? We gave you a key."

"I thought that was just while I was living here."

"No," I said, welcoming him. "Just come in."

"But if Simon or me are upstairs or something, shout up the stairs to let us know you're here," Mark said.

"Or something?" Sam smirked and waggled his eyebrows.

"Don't be cheeky," I made to cuff Sam's ear. He ducked.

Sam's expression grew serious. "I don't know what you said to Dad last night, but he came home and gave me a big hug. Then he went and had a long talk with Mum."

"I think he just realised what a lucky man he is to have such a terrific son," I said.

Sam looked perplexed.

"We told him we had grown really close to you. We also said what you'd said about you treating us like honorary dads. Hope you don't mind us telling him that," Mark said.

"'Course I don't."

"Thanks, mate." Mark gave him a hug.

Sam made to sit in his usual spot, but Mark stopped him.

"Just before you came round we'd decided to go to the garden centre. That back garden is in serious need of some TLC. I'm going to turn Simon into a gardener even if it kills me."

I pulled a face.

Sam giggled. "Can I come with you?"

"If it's all right with your mum and dad," I said. "I'd have thought they'd want to spend some time with their son not having seen him for a couple of weeks."

Sam's grin was back. "I'll go sort them out."

In the meantime Mark offered to *help* me into my coat.

"Give over." I slapped at his wandering hands. "Anyone would think we were teenagers."

"Who was it who said something about spring being when a young man's fancy turns to watching the sap rising?"

"Sap isn't the only thing that's rising," I said, squeezing Mark's crotch.

"Is this what you meant by 'or something?'" Sam asked, opening the front door.

I thumped Mark's arm. "Whose idea was it to tell him he didn't need to knock?"

I COULDN'T BELIEVE the range of plants, garden ornaments, furniture, and all the other stuff that was on sale at the garden centre. Not being green-fingered, I had never really taken much notice of such places.

Mark had suggested it would be nice if we ate some of our meals outside during the summer. I liked the idea. Although the wooden table and chair sets looked great, they weren't cheap, and we had nowhere to store such things out of the winter weather. I didn't like the look of white plastic. However, there was a special offer on a green plastic set that included a parasol and its base. My ever-present sense of Yorkshire thriftiness having been appeased by the reduced price, the three of us manhandled the large box onto our flat-bed trolley and continued shopping.

Mark explained that as the yard was mainly grass, he thought we'd be better off sticking to growing things in containers. We might dig up some of the lawn next year though. As I didn't have a clue, I let Mark decide what to get. We ended up with a couple of hanging baskets and some tubs.

Mark was like a kid in a sweet shop, putting this and that on the trolley. By the time we got to the checkout the trolley was piled high.

"How are we gonna get all this home?" Sam asked.

I was wondering the same thing.

"We sell roof racks," the young checkout operator smirked. "Aisle 17, about halfway down."

ONCE SAM RETURNED from his house with his dad's drill, Mark took charge of fixing up the brackets for the hanging baskets. We'd bought baskets that were already filled with plants. Mark said we'd fill them ourselves next year. I was thrilled to see him putting his own stamp on the place.

"Don't just stand there," Mark said when Sam and I were admiring our handiwork at setting up the table and chairs. "Give us a hand with these tubs."

"He's really getting into this," Sam said, lifting one end of a tub.

"I'm not looking forward to watering the things every day," I grumped taking the other end.

"Damn, we forgot to buy a hosepipe," Mark said. "And anyway, some of these plants won't need water every day. Although the baskets, and the…"

"I think the garden centre is open tomorrow, we'll get a hosepipe then," I interrupted, knowing despite what Mark said, we'd be watering every day.

"I'll go back with you," Sam volunteered. "You need one of those hoses on a reel, Granddad Bates has one. Besides, Alex, the cute guy on the checkouts, might be working again tomorrow."

I raised an eyebrow. "Alex? How come you know his name?"

"It was on his name badge."

I shook my head. "What about Billy?"

"Can he come, too? That'd be great," Sam said.

"You knew what I meant."

Sam grinned. "I can look, I just won't touch. Anyway, Billy's bum is nicer than Alex's."

Mark laughed.

Sam and I moved the last tub into its place to the right of the back door.

WE WERE RELAXING in the new chairs and discussing what to have for lunch when Sam said he thought he'd heard someone at the front door.

"If it's the Jehovah's—"

"Simon!" Mark warned.

"What?" Sam asked hovering by the back door.

"Never mind," I said. "Please go see who's at the front."

Sam soon returned with a stony-faced Mary.

"You look like you've lost a pound and found a penny," I said.

"Jerry!" she growled, flopping into the fourth seat at the table.

"Homemade lemonade?" Mark asked, lifting the pitcher.

"Thanks."

I waited until she'd taken her first drink before asking, "What about Jerry?"

"You remember I invited you to double date with us tonight?"

"Uh huh." In point of fact I'd forgotten.

"You told me to find out from Jerry if he'd be all right about it."

"Uh huh," I repeated, knowing what was coming next.

"He isn't. All right about it I mean."

I sighed, having guessed correctly.

"The bastard!" she growled.

Sam giggled.

"Sorry. Shouldn't have said that in front of you." Mary drained her glass and Mark filled it again.

"It's all right, you should hear my dad when he hits his thumb with his hammer."

Mary sent a brief smile Sam's way, then said, "Some of the things he…Jerry came out with!" she shuddered.

"I can imagine," Mark said, raising the pitcher again.

Mary shook her head. "Sadly, you probably can."

"We won't go out with you two if it'll save any unpleasantness. It doesn't matter," I said.

"It does matter, and there'll be no going out for any of us. I've dumped the lowlife, rat-faced, slimy bastard."

"That's a bit drastic." I took one of her hands and gave it a squeeze.

"I can't go out with someone who thinks like that." Mary sniffed back tears. It was obvious the argument with Jerry had really affected her. "How long have I known you?"

"About three years, give or take."

"You're my best friend. You're the kindest, most thoughtful and most all-round good guy I've ever met."

I lowered my head in embarrassment.

"Mark, if your partner wasn't gay, I'd have had him down the aisle so fast his feet wouldn't have touched the ground."

Sam giggled.

Mark got to his feet, came to stand behind my chair, and wrapped his arms around my shoulders. "He is gay, and he's spoken for." He kissed the top of my head.

My embarrassment increased. "Is it me, or has it suddenly got warmer out here?"

Back came Sam's giggles. "It's you."

"You two are perfect for each other," Mary sighed. "I thought Jerry was perfect for me."

"I'm sorry," I said softly.

"I told him he could stick his bigoted views up his arse."

Sam laughed.

"I'm sorry, I shouldn't sound off in front of you," Mary said to Sam.

"It's all right," Sam replied.

"Thanks."

Despite refusing it earlier, Mary filled her lemonade glass. She'd soon need the loo the way she was going.

Mark returned to his seat.

A satisfied smile spread across Mary's face.

"What?" I asked, surprised she'd be smiling at a time like this.

"Jerry and I had gone out in my car last night. I stormed out of the pub and drove home alone. I imagine the lowlife slime ball piece of shit had to get a taxi back to his parents' place."

"Good on you," Sam said.

"Yeah." She sighed yet again. "I'm glad I found out about him before we got any further in our relationship."

"That's something I suppose," I knew my comment would be of little comfort, but couldn't think of anything else to say.

"I need to get going," she announced, picking up her handbag. "Mind if I use your loo first?"

I smiled. "You know where it is."

In the house, just before she left, I said, "As I imagine you won't have plans for tonight, Mark and I are taking you out."

"Huh?"

"Simon's right," Mark said. "You need cheering up."

Mary thanked us and gave each of us—Sam including—a kiss.

"It's getting on for lunchtime," I told Sam once Mary had gone. "Shouldn't you be going home before your parents forget what you look like?"

Sam grumbled something about knowing where he wasn't wanted. But as he was smiling I knew he didn't mean it.

"Any more lip from you and," Mark held a clenched fist near Sam's face, "and...well I won't let you and Billy come with us to the garden centre tomorrow."

Sam's face broke into its customary grin. "Sorry."

"IT'S A SHAME," I said later that afternoon.

"What is?" Mark looked up from a seed catalogue he'd

picked up at the garden centre.

"Mary and Jerry. He seemed like a decent bloke. I'd have laid money on those two getting married and having two point four children, roses round the door, and all that."

Mark smiled. "You're such a romantic."

I spent the rest of the afternoon showing him just how romantic I was.

"IT'S NICE IN here," Mary said once we were seated in the restaurant.

"We came here with Sam the other day on our way back from Haworth," I explained, opening the menu.

"You think a lot of Sam."

"We do. He's a great kid," Mark said.

"When his dad did our loft conversion, it meant we could have him over for the odd night," I said, deciding on the spit-roast chicken.

As expected, the subject soon changed to the collapse of Mary and Jerry's relationship.

Mark told Mary we were sorry they'd split up, but Jerry was the one who had lost out.

"Thanks." She sighed. "It's true what they say. The best ones are either married or gay."

I smiled.

"I really thought he was Mr. Right, you know?"

I gave her hand a squeeze. "I know."

Mary talked, and I offered the occasional word of sympathy, knowing she needed to get it out of her system.

The waiter arrived and took our orders. Once he'd gone, a change of subject seemed in order. Mark got Mary to dish the dirt on my past friendship with her. This provided them with plenty of laughs at my expense. I didn't mind. The anecdotes brought back happy memories of when Mary and I worked together.

The food arrived and conversation all but ceased as we tucked in.

❖

IT WAS CHUCKING it down when I drew back the curtains Sunday morning.

"At least we won't need to water the plants today," Mark said as he looked at the dismal weather over my shoulder.

This reminded me we'd planned to go back to the garden centre.

We went downstairs and I started breakfast. I didn't say anything about how Sam wasn't around to cook it for us.

Once we'd eaten, I told Mark I'd drive to the garage to fill up and collect the Sunday papers.

WHEN I GOT back home, I could hear the vacuum cleaner working upstairs. Sam and Billy were sitting on the couch holding hands.

"Hi, Billy, how've you been?" I asked.

"I'm good. Thanks for letting me come with you today."

I shook my head. "We're only going to the garden centre. It won't be very exciting."

"Aren't you going to ask me how I am?" Sam pouted.

"No." I hung up my coat.

"Charming!" Sam said, letting go of Billy's hand and crossing his arms over his chest.

"I saw you only yesterday. I'd have seen the ambulance from here if you'd have been taken ill or something overnight." I ruffled Sam's hair.

"Geroff, I've just combed it."

I laughed. "Sorry, I forgot. We have to look nice for Adam."

"Alex," Sam corrected.

"Huh?" Billy looked at Sam.

"He works at the checkouts at the garden centre. But don't worry, he isn't a patch on you." Sam kissed Billy on the lips.

Billy smiled.

"Though I gotta say, Alex does have a nice arse," Sam added.

Billy punched Sam in the shoulder.

Just then the vacuum cleaner stopped, and shortly afterwards Mark came downstairs carrying it. "Ready to go see your other boyfriend, Sam?"

Sam harrumphed.

Laughing, Mark ruffled Sam's hair. "Sorry, mate."

"I've just combed it!" Sam protested again.

Both Billy and I were in stitches.

Mark looked at us in confusion.

"Never mind, my angel, I'll tell you later," I said.

"Uh, okay." Mark shook his head. "Let me put the Hoover away and we'll go."

I WAS SURPRISED how many people would want to visit a garden centre on a rainy Sunday morning. The car park was full, but eventually I managed to find a space a fair distance from the entrance.

"Looks like we'll be getting wet, lads," I said to the group.

The rain wasn't just wet, it was cold.

Once we'd made it inside, I turned to Mark. "Whose bright idea was it to buy a hosepipe in the rain?"

The two boys giggled.

It didn't take us long to find the hoses.

"Well, if it was up to me," Sam said, slapping a palm on one of the reels, "I'd go for this one. The hose is a bit thicker, so there's less chance of it kinking."

"And who appointed you the expert on garden hoses?" Mark asked, hands on hips.

"It's elementary, my dear Smith." Sam smiled back at him.

"Trust you to pick the most expensive one," I said, looking at the price tags on the different reels.

"Spoken like a true Yorkshireman," Sam laughed.

I sighed, and, knowing I was outnumbered, gave in.

Mark picked out a few bits and pieces he thought we might need. As it was still pouring it down outside, we delayed as long as we could. Sam showed interest in the water features, but I put my foot down.

"If I got one of those things the sound of it would have me wanting to visit the loo every five minutes."

Billy, who had been quiet up until this point, laughed.

Sam had hold of the reel as we headed toward the checkouts. There were two in operation. The first had two people in the queue, and the second, staffed by Alex, had three people waiting. Sam joined Alex's queue. I winked at Mark, who smiled back.

Although I had enough cash, I chose to pay by credit card knowing Alex would have to turn around to use the card-reading machine. Sam and Billy could barely suppress their giggles.

Back in the car, Mark asked, "Well, what's the verdict? Who has the cutest bum?"

We all laughed, but poor Billy went red. As the windows were steamed up, and no one could see in, Sam leaned over and gave Billy a kiss. "You have."

"Stop teasing the poor kid," I said once I'd got the giggles under control. I started the car and drove home.

When we were all back inside and had taken off our wet coats, Mark said, "I don't know what you want to do this morning, but it'll have to be something indoors."

"Monopoly!" Sam went to the drawer and pulled out the box.

Mark groaned. "Have we got time? When can we be rid, I mean, when do both your parents want you back?"

"Charming." Sam unfolded the board. "Mum said she'd have lunch on the table at one o'clock."

"I should be home for about then, too," Billy admitted.

❖

MARK WON THE game by a narrow margin. Sam took his defeat well, no doubt partly because Billy said he was impressed at how well Sam had played.

It came as no surprise that Sam decided to ride with me when I drove Billy home. Mark stayed at home to get lunch started. There was no argument about who should sit up front; they both chose the back seat.

When I returned home, dropping Sam off on the way, Mark had the vegetables peeled and the beef was in the oven.

"You didn't have to do all this," I said, coming up behind Mark and kissing his neck. "You get enough of that at work, not to mention you've usually got the dinner on when I get home every evening."

Mark turned around to face me and gave me a kiss. "I like cooking."

I returned his kiss. "Just so you know, you don't always have to."

"BLOODY TYPICAL!" I said, looking out of the kitchen window while doing the washing up after lunch. "We buy a load of garden furniture and it chucks it down."

"That's English weather for you," Mark replied, picking up the roasting pan and drying it.

Once everything was put away, we went back into the living room. I put Satie's *Gymnopédie* on the stereo and joined Mark on the sofa.

I sighed. "I love listening to this while watching the raindrops streak down the window."

Mark nuzzled my neck. "Like I said before, you're such a romantic."

Chapter 9

OUR LIVES SETTLED into a comfortable routine. We saw a fair bit of Sam, and more likely than not, Billy was with him, too.

ONE SUNDAY EVENING after dinner the phone rang. Mark and I were in our usual positions on the sofa. Mark got up and answered it.

"Hello? Oh, hi, Mrs…Gran."

I smiled; I could just imagine her telling Mark to call her Gran.

"Do you want to talk to Simon?" Mark looked over at me. "Okay, thanks. No, we've nothing much on next weekend I don't think. Hang on, I'll ask." Mark lowered the receiver and turned to me. "It'll be okay if your Gran comes over this weekend?"

"Of course."

"Yeah, Gran, you're more than welcome. Do you want to go anywhere special with us?" He absent-mindedly scratched his stomach. "Okay then…I'm sure we can do that. Hang on I'll put him on." Mark handed the phone to me.

"Hi, Gran, how are you?"

"Mustn't grumble. Though this damp weather isn't helping with my rheumatism."

"Sorry to hear that." I knew Gran's pain had to be bad for her to have mentioned it. "What about those new pills the doctor gave you?"

Gran promised she'd give them another try. Then she launched into a story about what was happening at the old-folks' community centre.

"I was thinking about staying with you from Friday to Monday if that's okay."

"Of course it's okay. You're welcome any time."

"I'll probably be spending most of the time with my friends, but do you fancy going somewhere nice for lunch on May Day Monday?"

"Yeah. That sounds nice. I'll think of somewhere and book a table."

We said our goodbyes, but before I could get back to the sofa, the telephone rang again. This time it was my mother.

"Hi, Mum, how are you?"

"I'm fine, and your dad sends his love. He's working of course. Some demonstration going on in the city centre I think."

"Sounds typical."

Dad was a police inspector and they often called upon him at the last minute to come into work.

"Yes, and in this weather, I hope he's managed to get somewhere dry."

I sighed inwardly when we were reduced to talking about the weather so soon in our conversation. I'd exhausted the topic of my promotion a few weeks earlier, so I had to scrabble around for the next few minutes to try and find other things to say. When the silences became too frequent we ended the call. I'm sure Mum was as relieved as I was that our weekly mother-son contact had been gotten through once again. Things were okay with my parents, we just weren't very close. They accepted my homosexuality, but we had a silent agreement that it wouldn't be discussed.

"Want to see what's on the telly?" Mark asked after I'd ended the call.

I walked over and turned the set on. Using the remote control, I flipped through the channels. There was a documentary about polar bears, so we resumed our cuddle and watched it.

GRAN'S VISIT WAS full of laughter and joy. She was delighted to learn that Miss Finch, her old neighbour, was telling stories to the youngsters at the library.

"I think she makes half of them up, but she's a natural teller of tales," Gran said.

"I put my head around the door the other day…she had them all sat round her in a semi-circle and every single face was turned up to her as she told them about the time she was on fire-watch duty in Leeds during the Blitz," I said.

"That's one of Maggie's best stories," Gran admitted.

Although Gran spent much of her time out and about during her visit, we still saw a good deal of her and, as we'd promised, we took her to lunch on Bank Holiday Monday. Harry had recommended a pub on the way to Leeds, so Gran drove her car and I followed at a more sedate pace in mine.

After lunch, we bade each other a fond farewell, and we promised to make a return visit to Leeds sometime in the summer.

"That lady is an absolute scream," Mark said on the way home.

I smiled and flipped on the indicator to turn right.

"She seemed to like the room."

"I knew she would, she's not one for chintzy curtains and the rest, which is just as well because I hate that sort of thing." The traffic cleared and I made the turn.

"Me, too."

"Trust her to make a joke about how she hadn't expected anything else from two gay men."

"I know," Mark said. "I just wish she hadn't said it in the middle of the pub."

"That's Gran. But at least no one knew us there." I turned into our street.

"True."

Not long after getting home there was a knock on the door.

"Can I come in?"

I was about to tell Sam that he didn't need to ask, but one look at the kid's distressed face had the words dying on my lips. I ushered him in and closed the door.

We hadn't seen all that much of Sam during the holiday weekend what with Gran's visit and Sam's own family commitments.

Sam's distress increased so Mark put his arms around him.

"What's happened?" I asked.

"My grandma and granddad Bates." Sam took a calming breath. "We've just come back. They started talking about Uncle Steve…Saying nasty things. He sniffed. "But it was worse than usual and I got upset."

"Sorry, mate." Mark rubbed Sam's back.

"When they asked me what was wrong I…I told them I was gay, too and they shouldn't say stuff like that."

"Oh." I wondered if he'd made the right decision to come out, but quickly realised it didn't matter if it was right or wrong, he'd done it.

"It got pretty ugly," Sam was continuing.

"I'm so sorry," I said.

Dad and Mum were great though," Sam smiled a little. "As we were leaving Dad told them we wouldn't be back until they apologised to me."

I knew that wouldn't have been an easy decision for Paul and Helen to have to make. But good on them for sticking up for their son. My opinion of Paul and Helen, already high, increased.

"Let's hope your grandparents see sense," I said, though doubted it'd happen any time soon.

"Yeah, right." Sam sniffed.

"Unfortunately there are people in this world who can't or won't understand us. We just have to rise above the hate and try and get on with our lives," I said, rubbing Sam's shoulder.

"It's so unfair though. They're my grandparents."

"I know," Mark said. "But Simon's right, you have to rise above it. I know it's not easy, but you can't let them win."

"And your grandparents are the ones who will lose out the most," I put in, "because they won't get to know what a great person their grandson is."

Sam soon collected himself. Mark went over to the Bates' house to tell them Sam was safe and with us.

When Mark returned and said Sam's parents were okay about him staying the evening, Sam got out of his chair and, much to my surprise, came and sat between Mark and me on the sofa.

Mark told Sam a funny story about a girl he knew at school who kept pestering him for a date. "I went out with her a couple of times."

"Really?" Sam said.

I wondered the same myself.

"Yeah. I only did it so I could go to her house. I fancied her older brother something rotten."

This got Sam laughing, although I felt a twinge of jealousy; stupid because I didn't even know Mark back then.

SAM STAYED WITH us for the rest of the day; we fed him, and didn't let him go home until it was his bedtime. Mark and I walked him back to his house, even though it was only a couple of doors down.

Helen invited us in when we arrived.

"Feeling better now?" she asked, touching Sam's cheek.

"Yeah. Mark and Simon were great."

We smiled at him.

"Thanks," Helen said to us and offered us a cup of coffee.

"It's okay, we just had one."

Paul came into the room; I think he'd been checking on Charlotte. "Hey guys. Everything all right now?"

Sam nodded, then yawned.

"Think it's about your bedtime." Paul patted Sam's shoulder.

"Uh huh." Sam stifled another yawn.

I was surprised he was agreeing to go to bed so willingly, not that he ever put up too much of a fuss when he'd stayed with us. But then he'd had quite an emotional day and was most probably tired out.

Once Sam had given everyone a goodnight hug and gone upstairs, Paul turned to us. "Helen and I have been talking, haven't we, love?"

Helen nodded.

"With your permission we want to make a change to our wills." I'm sure my mouth opened, but before I could say anything Paul continued. "If anything should happen to us while the kids are still growing up, we'd like to think there was someone out there who could take care of them."

"Uh, yeah," Mark said.

"I know this is coming at you suddenly, and you can take as much time to think about it as you need, but should the worst happen, would you two be willing to take on the responsibility?"

Stunned, I looked over at Mark, who seemed to be in a similar state.

"Erm, yeah," I said, as much to fill the silence as anything.

"It's a bit gruesome to think of things like that," Mark put in. "But I understand you need to sort stuff like this out."

Paul nodded.

"But what about friends, members of your family?" Mark asked.

"Most of our friends already have kids and they wouldn't have room for two more," Helen said. "Paul's mum and dad are getting on in years and I doubt they'd be able to cope. And my parents…"

I nodded.

"Not that either of us have any plans to bite the dust anytime soon," Paul chuckled. "But it'd be a weight off our minds if we knew things would be taken care of if the worst were to happen."

"We understand," I said, recovering sufficiently from the shock to answer.

"Like I said, you don't have to make any decisions now," Paul reminded.

Helen smiled at us. "Want that coffee now?"

I nodded. "I think we need it."

I HAD A pleasant walk to work the next morning. Spring had definitely sprung. The tubs of flowers, which the Council had put out in the high street, were coming into bloom. The plants Mark had bought for our garden were also doing well. He spent ages tending to them, and they were responding to his ministrations. The lawn was also looking much healthier than I'd ever seen it.

I entered the library, signed in and chatted with a few members of staff. Amazingly Mary was in early.

"How was your Bank Holiday?" I asked, wondering how she was holding up.

"Not bad." She smiled. "I think I might get back with Jerry."

"Oh?"

I didn't know whether Jerry had softened his stance on

homosexuality or if Mary had just decided that they would go on despite Jerry's views. I hoped for the former, but it really wasn't any of my business.

"Jerry decided to get himself educated." Mary said.

"Huh?" Jerry was a post-graduate history student at York University.

"He's getting educated about his homophobia."

"Ah." I nodded.

"It seems there's some kind of gay, lesbian and bisexual awareness group at the university, and Jerry has been going along to some of their meetings to find out what things are really like."

Maybe Jerry really was serious about working on his prejudices.

"I hope it all works out for you, we all deserve to be happy in love, and I know I am," I smiled.

"Everything still rosy in the garden then?"

I laughed. "Funny you should mention gardening. I was looking at the flowers in the high street on my way in this morning."

"I hope the vandals don't go round and cut the heads off all the flowers this year."

That had happened a couple of years back. There had been a flood of angry letters from the 'hang them and flog them' brigade to the editor of the *Littleborough Gazette* over it.

"Well," I sighed, "this won't help me scale the paper mountain."

"And I better go and get things organised in the department. John is really working out now he's been made permanent."

"Glad to hear it," I said as I got behind my desk.

I'd been invited onto the interview panel for that post. It was fascinating to see things from the other side. There had been a couple of decent candidates. Although I couldn't tell Mary, John hadn't been our first choice. We'd offered the position to a graduate, but he declined the offer as he'd accepted a job nearer his hometown. I wasn't sure why he still went for the position here, but I guessed that was his business. John was doing pretty well by all accounts, so I was happy we were able to keep him on.

Miss Finch's sessions were proving very popular with the little ones. Some of the mothers were sitting in on the stories, too. I was glad the storytelling was working out, as it was the first project I'd initiated on getting the promotion. If things had gone wrong, I couldn't help but feel that it would have reflected badly on me.

At lunchtime I headed to Daphne's as usual. I got myself seated and was deciding what to order when Mark came to my table.

I smiled up at him. "The nice weather must have brought out the shoppers," I said, looking over the almost full tables.

"Yeah."

I hated that the crowds forced us to hide our feelings for each other.

Mark bent closer and pointed to something on the menu. Speaking quietly, he said, "Daphne said I could take the second week off in August. I know I haven't worked here that long, but I still qualify for holiday entitlement."

"That's great." More quietly, I said, "I'll see if I can get the same week off, too. We'll talk more about it later."

Mark nodded and flipped open his order pad. "So that's one Caesar salad with extra anchovies. Anything to drink?"

I glowered at him. Mark knew I hated anchovies.

"And one Diet Coke. Coming right up." He closed his pad and left, a grin on his beautiful face.

BACK AT THE library, as I digested my Caesar salad—that had come without anchovies—I placed a call to the town hall. It seemed as long as there was a senior librarian at another branch who was at the other end of the phone in case of emergencies, I could take my leave whenever I wanted. So I rang around and a couple of my senior librarian counterparts agreed to cover for me if necessary. I was confident my staff could cope in my absence. Generally August was a quiet month. Things wouldn't start to hot up until the new academic year began in September and October.

In the past I hadn't done much about holidays. I would take off the odd day and organise a few trips to museums or sites of historical interest. I'd come home that same evening or stay at Gran's or my parents' house. However, with Mark, we could plan something much more exciting.

"LUCY, I'M HOME," I called out as usual when I came through the front door.

"Hi." Mark greeted me with a kiss. "You look pleased with yourself."

"I managed to get the same week off work as you."

"That's great. We'll have to go to the travel agents and get some ideas."

"Don't know what'll be available this late in the season. Have you got a passport?" I asked.

"Yeah, I remembered to take it when I left home."

I gave him a squeeze to help ease his bad memories of his unpleasant departure.

"Do you think Paul and Helen will let Sam come with us?" we both said at the same time, making us laugh.

We had dinner, did the washing up, then went back into the living room and I put on some music. However, neither of us could settle.

"Are you thinking what I'm thinking?" Mark asked.

"You mean should we go round to Sam's and see if he can come on holiday with us?"

"We're like a couple of school kids asking the parents of a friend if their son can come out to play."

I laughed.

HELEN LET US in.

"We're not interrupting anything are we?" I asked.

"No, no. Come on through," she said, leading the way. "We were just watching the evening news. Do you want a cuppa?"

"No thanks," Mark answered for both of us.

The Bates only had instant coffee and I'd gotten Mark to appreciate real coffee.

Paul switched off the TV with the remote and stood to greet us. "If you're after Sam he's just upstairs finishing his homework."

"No, it's you we want to see." Mark said. "Well, erm, we'd like you to do us a favour, well I suppose we're doing you a favour, too…" He ground to a halt.

Paul looked confused. "Take a seat and start from the beginning," he smiled.

"What my partner here is trying to say is that we've booked a week's leave in August and were thinking about going away, and we were hoping you'd let us take Sam with us," I said.

Mark cut in before Paul could say anything. "That is if you haven't planned on going anywhere yourself, I thought with it being summer and everything, you wouldn't be able to get the time off."

Paul smiled at our little double act. He looked over at Helen, who was also smiling. "Where were you thinking of going?"

"We hadn't got that far yet. Probably somewhere in Europe. It all depends what the travel agents have left," I said.

Paul shrugged. "We better ask the boy himself." He smiled. "Play along with me if you will." He went upstairs.

Within a minute Sam came bouncing into the living room

and greeted us, Paul following a few steps behind.

"I said you wouldn't be interested," Paul said, putting on a serious expression, "but Simon and Mark insisted on asking you anyway." He paused for a few moments for dramatic effect.

"What?" Sam looked from his dad to Mark and me, then back to his dad.

"They're thinking about going abroad for a week in August, and they were wondering if you wanted to tag along with them. But like I said, I didn't think you'd be interested."

It only took Sam a couple of seconds before he launched himself at the pair of us. "Can I?"

"I take it that's a 'yes' then?" Paul smiled.

"You bet!" Sam replied eagerly. "Where are we going?"

I shrugged. "You can help us choose."

"Cool!" Sam said. "Have you got any brochures?"

"No, we only found out today we could have the time off," Mark told him. "But it's my half day tomorrow, so I'll go into Simmons and pick some up. How's that?"

"Cool!" Sam repeated.

"When you book it, mention my name," Paul said. "I did some work for the owner last year. Hopefully you'll get a good deal."

"Thanks for that," I said.

By the time we were ready to leave the Bates' house, Sam was almost bouncing off the walls, so much so Helen insisted Sam go upstairs and pack an overnight bag.

"It's your fault for making him so excited," she smiled at us, "so you can put up with his noise. If he stays here he'll wake Charlotte."

Whilst Sam was upstairs, Paul turned to us. "It's good of you two to think of him. He'd have missed out on a holiday this year otherwise."

"We'll enjoy taking him," Mark said.

I nodded in agreement.

Sam was downstairs again in a flash.

"Have you packed your PE kit?" Helen asked.

"Yes, Mum."

"Right then, let's go, and give your mum and dad some peace," I told Sam as we left the house.

Back at our place, Mark asked, "Do you want me to pick you up after school, and we can go and get some brochures?"

"Ace!" Then Sam's grin faded. "But wouldn't that be out of your way?"

"That's okay, anything to oblige." Mark gave a bow, and Sam giggled.

"It'll be great going on holiday with you two." Sam beamed.

"We'll enjoy it, too," I said. "I don't think we'd be able to take Billy though. His parents wouldn't understand why complete strangers were asking to take their son away."

"That's all right. I think he'll be on holiday then anyway."

Feeling myself getting into the holiday spirit I said, "When we decide where we're going, I'll borrow some language tapes from the library, and we can practice a few simple phrases."

"Ooh, I can't wait," Sam said.

"Well, you'll have to, we're not going for another three months," I told him.

"I know, I know," Sam sighed.

"Never mind," Mark soothed, "It'll give you plenty of time to learn what 'you've got a nice bum' is in French, German and…"

Sam leapt on top of Mark and the two began to wrestle.

WHEN I GOT home the next evening, I found Mark and Sam in the kitchen, brochures and leaflets spread over the table.

"Where's my dinner?" I said with mock anger.

Sam giggled.

"Have you decided where we're going?" I set up the coffee maker and started it going.

"We were waiting for you." Mark stood, hugged me, and

gave me a kiss.

"Thanks, angel. I think the budget will only stretch to somewhere in Europe. Besides, if we're just going for the week, we don't want somewhere too far off."

"Amsterdam looks great," Sam piped up. "Plenty of gay activities."

Mark shrugged. "Wouldn't you want somewhere with a sandy beach and all that?"

"Probably," Sam admitted.

I threw together a few leftovers as the others continued to suggest possible destinations.

Once we'd eaten, the serious business of making a decision of where to go began.

"The South of France looks nice," I said.

"It's a bit pricey," Mark admitted.

"You sure you weren't born in Yorkshire?" Sam giggled.

Mark smiled. "What about Spain?" he asked.

Brochures were found and pages turned.

"There's a lot of choice," I admitted.

"Why don't we look at it from a different angle then?" Sam suggested.

"What do you mean?" I asked.

"Have you got a large piece of paper and a felt tip or marker pen?"

I found the requested items.

"Now we make a list." Sam uncapped the marker pen. "The things at the top should be absolutes. Things we all want out of the holiday. Then we put things we would like, but could live without. We then go down to things that would be nice, but we're not that bothered about."

"You're not just a pretty face, are ya?" Mark pinched Sam's cheek.

"Geroff," Sam said, but he was beaming.

We talked about each item before Sam wrote it down. We all decided we wanted a family type holiday, somewhere fairly quiet, near a beach, pretty scenery, not too overly developed, and places of historical interest to visit. This last was my and Sam's suggestion, but Mark was also willing.

"Now we hit the brochures again," Sam said.

A few minutes later Mark slapped the table. Eureka!"

"Okay, Archimedes, what have you discovered?" I asked.

Sam giggled at my joke, but I don't think Mark got it.

"A self-catering apartment just outside Ciutadella on the island of Menorca." He showed us the page, we read it and we liked it.

"Yup, that fits the bill," I said, checking Sam's list.

Sam pinched Mark's cheek. "You're not just a pretty face, are ya?"

"THERE'S A SECOND-FLOOR self-catering apartment free during the week you wanted," the woman at the travel agent's said. "All the buildings in that area are low-rise. They aren't allowed to build any higher than three storeys."

She showed us a series of pictures. It all looked very nice. The apartment blocks seemed spaced well apart and not overlooked by taller buildings.

"Nude bathing on the balcony," Sam whispered in my ear.

I nudged him in the ribs. "Shush!"

"As you can see, the apartments have one bedroom and the settee in the lounge converts into a second bed," she continued, thankfully unaware of Sam's comment.

"Good," I said, noticing the double bed in the picture of the bedroom. I wondered if she knew Mark and I were a couple.

"A small supermarket is on site, though there's a hypermarket within walking distance."

"Are there any organised tours of the Island?" Sam asked, no doubt remembering our wish to explore historic buildings and the like.

"Yes," she nodded. "The tour rep at the apartment complex will have all those details."

"You seem pretty knowledgeable about the place," I remarked.

"My parents bought a house there a few years ago. Now they're retired they live on the island for about six months of the year. For the most part Menorca isn't spoilt by over-development, unlike Majorca."

We continued to look at the pictures, though I was already sold on the idea.

"Like I said, you're lucky we still have something like this available especially in August," the lady said.

It was time to make up our minds. I looked at Mark who nodded. A quick look over at Sam's smile let me know his opinion.

Turning back to the travel agent, I said, "Sign us up, please."

Chapter 10

THE REST OF the spring and early summer flew by, Sam crossing every day off on his wall calendar.

As expected, Mary got back with Jerry. He had realised, much to Mary's relief, that gay people didn't have horns growing out of their heads. He also learnt that not all gay people were limp-wristed or spoke with a lisp. We did go out on a double date. It was okay, but I wouldn't put it any higher than that. Jerry behaved himself, no cross words or dirty looks were exchanged, but once it was over, Mark and I agreed it was an experience we weren't keen to repeat. Pity, because Jerry was very attractive, and there was no doubt he doted on Mary.

One Sunday Mark answered the phone. It was my mother and, after a few words were exchanged, he handed the phone to me.

Once we'd greeted each other and my mother had told me what she and Dad had gotten up to and I'd told her what had happened at work as well as the plot of the latest book I'd been reading, the expected silence fell.

Then she asked, "This Mark. Are you and he serious?"

The question surprised me, as my sexuality was a subject she generally avoided. I was honest with her and told her that Mark "was my life."

She seemed to take the statement well, because her next comment was, "Your father and I were thinking about coming to see you next weekend for your birthday. Would it be convenient?"

I had a brief word with Mark, then told Mum we'd love to have them come. A slight exaggeration, but I would be pleased to see them nonetheless.

My birthday fell on Friday, 12 June, and by happy circumstance, Mark's was two days later.

Mum took a while to warm to Mark, but by the time she and Dad left on Sunday afternoon, they were getting on pretty well. They even swapped a few jokes. I was amazed, though really shouldn't have been. My man could charm the birds off the trees if he set his mind to it.

Dad took to Mark straight away. They had a common interest in gardening, and they spent a fair bit of the weekend out in the backyard. Mark asked Dad's advice on what to do if we dug up some of the lawn next year. All-in-all their visit went better than I'd thought it would.

"Your mum is nice, but she's very different from your Gran," Mark said to me in bed the night my parents left.

"I used to pull Gran's leg about how she must have picked up the wrong baby from the maternity ward."

Mark chuckled.

"Trouble is, Gran gave birth to Mum at home."

His chuckle turned into a full-on laugh. Despite my mother's apparent acceptance of my sexuality, I'd still been on eggshells around her all weekend, being careful not to hug or kiss Mark in her presence. Now I was free to touch and kiss him as much as I wanted, and I took full advantage.

"Frisky," Mark said when my hand strayed below the waistband of his sleep shorts.

"Complaining?"

He wasn't, and he proved it…twice.

THE CROSSES ON Sam's calendar finally reached Friday, 7 August.

Paul and Helen agreed Sam should spend the night at our house because we had to leave for Manchester airport at an ungodly hour Saturday morning to be in time for our 7.15 a.m. flight.

The bell on the alarm clock started ringing. It was over on Mark's side of the bed and, after a pause, he reached over and silenced it.

"Whose idea was it to get an early flight?" he croaked.

"It was the only one they had with seats still available."

Mark yawned. "Mind if I use the loo first?"

"No problem. I'll go wake up Sam." I climbed the stairs to the second bedroom. "You awake?" I asked through a jaw-splitting yawn.

"I was too excited to sleep."

"You might be able to get forty winks on the plane." I scratched at my jaw. I'd need to shave before we set out.

"I don't want to miss anything."

"Uh huh." I turned to leave, wondering if Mark had finished in the bathroom.

"EVERYONE'S GOT THEIR passports and money, and you've got the tickets, Simon?" Mark asked.

"Yep, all present and correct." I rubbed at my eyes.

"Well, if we've forgotten it, it's staying forgotten," Mark

said as he locked the front door.

Sam had decided he wanted to ride up front. I don't think Mark minded much. He could stretch out in the back seat and perhaps catch a quick nap.

I hadn't had much practice at driving on motorways, but there was little traffic on the M62 over the Pennines at that time in the morning.

We were early for check-in, I hated leaving things till the last minute, and so we didn't have to queue for too long.

"Did you pack your bag yourself, sir?" the woman at the desk asked me when we got to the head of the line.

No, I met a shifty-looking man with a long beard in the street and he packed for me. He told me that if I heard any ticking noises coming from the case, not to worry about it, I thought. "Yes, I packed the case myself." I said aloud.

She asked a few more dumb questions, and took my suitcase. She did the same things for Mark and Sam. I'd told Mark not to pack a tube of lube; I didn't mind us taking condoms, but I'd had visions of a burley customs officer x-raying our cases and finding some KY. Hopefully we'd be able to buy what we needed over there. Mark had laughed at my caution.

We had plenty of time to potter around the airport. Sam thought he saw someone famous from the telly, but I told him not to make a fuss, as they wouldn't appreciate being accosted at five a.m.

Sam shrugged. "I don't like the character he plays anyway."

None of us had felt like eating anything at home. However, I'd developed a bit of an appetite now I was more awake. The others seemed to be in a similar state. Getting something to eat would also help pass the time.

Sam wanted to load up his plate.

"I wouldn't eat too much, mate," Mark said. "If you're... unwell on the plane, you'll have a lot more to come up."

"Okay, I'll just have some cereal and a sausage sandwich."

The sandwich sounded good, so I got one as well. Mark decided he'd go Continental and chose a croissant, some fresh fruit, and a yoghurt.

"You might as well get into the spirit of things, because this is what we'll be eating when we get there," he told our bemused teenager.

Sam grinned. "I think I'll wait till we get there."

After we ate, I had a quick look round the bookshops.

"You can take the boy out of the library, but you can't take the library out of the boy," Mark said.

"Less of the 'boy' if you don't mind," I grumbled, picking up a Stephen King paperback and, intrigued by the cover image, began to read the blurb on the back.

Armed with the book and some boiled sweets, I walked to the bored-looking shop assistant who was leaning against the cash register yawning into her hand.

Still having lots of time to kill we wandered into the departures lounge, found seats and listened to the announcements for flights going to various exotic and not so exotic locations. I started my book and Mark took Sam to the observation area to see the planes taking off and landing.

THE ANNOUNCEMENT WENT out that our flight was ready for boarding. But where was Sam? He'd gone to the toilet, but that had been ten minutes before. I started to panic.

"It's okay, here he is," Mark said. "And we've still got plenty of time."

We made our way to the gate, and after a bit more waiting around, we were able to get on the plane. I'd read an article about the dangers of deep-vein thrombosis, so wondered aloud to Mark if I should have gotten us compression stockings.

Smiling indulgently at me, he said, "Flying to Spain isn't exactly long-haul."

"Suppose."

Discreetly taking my hand, Mark gave it a squeeze. "Stop worrying."

I smiled at him and squeezed his hand back.

Fortunately, we'd been given a row of three seats together. Sam wanted to be by the window. I didn't mind where I sat as long as I was next to Mark, so I took the middle seat.

Handlers eventually pushed the plane back from the gate and it began to taxi. I watched the stewardesses give their safety talk, feeling compelled to check under my seat that the tab to pull out the life-jacket was indeed there.

"Stop worrying," Mark said.

"Sorry." I sat up straight and tried to keep my hands from shaking.

Mark laid a comforting hand over mine. "If I'd have known you'd be this nervous I'd have suggested taking a holiday in Britain."

"Sorry," I said again. "I'll be okay once we're in the air."

The taxiing seemed to take an age.

"You don't think we're going to ride all the way to Menorca on the ground?" Sam asked.

"We'd get a bit wet once we got to the English Channel," Mark told him.

The speed of the aircraft increased, so did the noise of the engines and the vibrations in the cabin. Mark took my left hand in his right. I closed my eyes and offered up a quick prayer.

THE PLANE FINALLY began to level off, and we were told we could loosen our seatbelts.

"Are you and Mark going to go to the loo together?" Sam whispered in my ear. "You know, join the mile high club?"

I sent him a withering look, which had no effect on the wattage of his grin. If I thought I could get away with it, I would take Mark to the toilet and…

"Just wait till I tell your mother that you know about things like that," Mark said.

Sam shrugged. "Mum and Dad probably did it on the flight to Gran Canaria."

I tried to push away images of a heterosexual sex act being performed in a confined place. My stomach was unsettled enough as it was.

Just then an announcement came over the loudspeaker telling us that the cabin staff would pass among us with headsets so we could listen to the in-flight entertainment. All three of us decided that we'd get sets. As Mark was in the aisle seat, he gave the male flight attendant the money. After giving us our headsets and smiling at Sam, the man continued up the aisle.

Sam leaned over to me and whispered, "Do you think he's gay? The way he walks and everything."

I had to admit, he did have a bit of a swishy walk. "Probably. Why, did you want to ask him?" I reached for the call button above Sam's seat.

Sam batted at my hand. "No!"

Sam then decided to fiddle around with the entertainment console built into the arm of his seat. I connected my headphones to my console and found a channel playing some relaxing classical music. Closing my eyes, I reclined the seat. Suddenly the music changed to heavy metal and the volume increased. My eyes shot open, I ripped off the headphones and sat bolt upright in my seat.

"Sorry, I must have pressed the wrong button," Sam laughed.

"Mark can sit in the middle on the flight home," I grumped, settling back in the seat.

The flight attendants began to serve breakfast. I expected something inedible. However, I was pleasantly surprised. The bread roll was fresh, the coffee hot and strong, but the best part was the hot foil packet. It contained a sausage, fried potatoes, and scrambled eggs. The latter were beautifully light and creamy.

The rest of the flight passed without incident. Mark and I did visit the toilets, but much to Sam's disappointment, we went separately.

Finally the announcement was given to put up our tray tables, bring our seats to their upright positions and fasten our seatbelts. My nerves started to get the better of me again. I was all right during the flight, it was just the take-off and landing bits I could do without.

The plane began to tilt forward. This time I didn't reach for Mark's hand. Eventually I heard the tires make contact with the runway. We were warned the engine noise would increase due to reverse thrust; I knew that, but the noise was still unsettling. Our speed slowed, we taxied for quite a while, and then we stopped.

I knew most of the passengers would try to bolt for the exits as soon as they could. I told Sam that we might as well stay in our seats, as it would be a few minutes before we could leave. He agreed, though I could tell he was eager to be off.

Unlike in Manchester, we had to walk down a set of metal stairs to get out of the aircraft. The heat hit me like a solid wall as soon as I stepped out of the plane. However, I quickly recovered, and we made our way to the shuttle bus.

Passing through customs was a formality. I don't think the man did more than glance at my passport. A good thing too, because like most passport photos, it was pretty terrible. The usual arrival routines and transfer to the resort passed without incident. The bus dropped us outside the lobby of the apartment complex. The driver removed our cases from the luggage compartment under the bus, and we made our way, along with the other guests who had just arrived, into the air-conditioned interior.

As everyone waited to check in the tour rep began his welcoming speech.

"Hello, I'm Peter, and this is my friend Patrick…"

I was transported back in time to Sunday afternoons at Gran's house. We would listen to re-runs of classic radio comedy shows such as Round the Horne. Peter's choice of words, and his mode of delivery, sounded just like Hugh Paddick in the Julian and Sandy sketches.

"...and we would like to welcome you chaps and chapesses to the start of your holiday here on the beautiful Island of Menorca."

He kept rattling on when all I wanted to do was get to our apartment and start my holiday. I prayed Sam wouldn't make a comment about Peter acting gay. Luck was smiling down on me because, although he smirked, he kept his mouth shut.

However, my luck didn't hold. When we got to the head of the line of guests checking in I gave the young Spanish girl our tickets, she looked at them, consulted her register and said in passable English, "Afraid is mistake."

Oh no! I thought. *We've been double-booked.* I imagined having to go from apartment complex to hotel to boarding house to find a bed.

She continued at what I thought was a slightly louder volume, "Meester Peters and Meester Smith, your apartment has double bed."

"That's okay," I said quietly, not wanting to draw too much attention to us.

She shook her head. "Double bed for man and wife. But we all full."

"It's fine," I said through gritted teeth. Sam and Mark were of little help, they were trying, not all that successfully, to remain straight-faced.

"Can I be of assistance?" Peter swished over.

"Yes, I was just telling the young lady that the apartment we've booked is okay," I said, sending up a silent prayer that this whole scene would soon be over.

Peter and the receptionist held a conversation in rapid-fire Spanish with accompanying hand gestures. Peter gave Mark and me a long look over, came to a decision, and then continued conversing with the confused woman. She blushed, then presented us with the register which Mark and I signed. She then handed over the room key without meeting our eyes. Whereas Peter on the other hand gave us a smile and a knowing wink.

I got us out of there as quickly as dignity permitted, not helped by Mark and Sam who were practically incapable of walking due to their now unsuppressed laughter.

"I knew I should have let you deal with check-in," I told Mark, giving him a hard stare.

After getting lost a couple of times we located our apartment block and climbed the stairs to the top floor...there was no lift. I inserted the key in the lock to our apartment's front door and turned the handle. Mercifully the door opened and we walked in. I made sure the door was locked behind us.

"God, I hate scenes like that," I said, accepting Mark's hug.

"I know, but you did really well."

"I don't think we left Peter in much doubt about our situation."

"So?"

I released myself from Mark and flopped on the couch from where I watched Sam explore the small apartment. He looked in every cupboard and drawer, and not surprisingly came up empty. However, the fridge yielded a couple of bottles of water, juice and a small carton of milk. He then went on to examine the French windows that led onto the balcony.

"Hey, there's even French windows in the bathroom," his echo-y voice announced from there.

In fact the whole apartment echoed, the walls being whitewashed brick and the floor covered in white ceramic tile. I guessed this was to help keep the place cool. Unlike the reception area, the apartment didn't seem to be air-conditioned. Each of the French windows had slatted metal shutters on the outside. Sam soon realised you could close the shutters but leave the doors open, thus getting the benefit of any breeze, but without sunlight.

"It's nice," he finally concluded, coming back into the living room area and flopping on the wood-framed sofa between

Mark and me.

Mark ruffled Sam's hair. "Glad you approve."

"Don't fancy having French windows in the bog though," Sam added.

"You'll have to remember to close the shutters beforehand," I laughed.

Sam soon got up again and went out onto the balcony. He came back in through another door. "Hey, it's on two sides," he announced. "You can see loads, just like in those pictures that woman showed us."

"Want to sunbathe nude?" Mark asked, reminding Sam of what he'd said in the travel agent's office.

"Uh, no." Sam blushed and fired back, "But you can if you want."

"Yeah, might do later. Help me get an all-over tan."

"Really?" Sam's eyes fixed on Mark.

Mine swivelled that way, too.

"Well, we'll see." Mark ducked his head.

"This won't get things organised," I said, standing and taking my suitcase into the bedroom.

Unzipping my case, I found my bag of toiletries and took it, along with a towel and a change of clothes, into the bathroom.

Shower finished, I came back into the living room where Sam had made coffee.

"Thanks," I said, accepting a cup. "You remembered to use bottled water?"

Sam nodded. "But it's instant coffee."

I tasted it. "Not bad, thanks. Once we're settled in we'll take a walk to the resort's supermarket and buy a few groceries."

"I'M GLAD WE'VE got a double bed," Mark said, joining me in the bedroom after his shower.

"I wouldn't have wanted to have to share a twin bed with you."

"Dunno." Mark waggled his eyebrows. "Might have been fun having to squeeze together."

I smiled and gave him a kiss.

Mark sighed. "This is the first real holiday I've had since leaving home."

"I know."

Mark stayed quiet, just lazily running a hand up and down my back as I snuggled up to him.

The moment was broken when Sam yelled, "I can't flush the bog!"

Mark sighed. "The price of having children."

I laughed and got up to investigate.

"See?" I showed an incredulous Sam how he needed to lift the small plunger on top of the water tank then let it fall.

Chapter 11

THE THREE OF us decided to seek out the supermarket to stock up on breakfast items and other necessities. We'd discussed our meal arrangements months earlier. We'd planned to eat breakfast in the apartment, but have most of our other meals out. The brochures had said there were loads of restaurants and cafés dotted about the area.

"Damn!" Mark stared at the locked door to the supermarket. "They're closed for siesta."

We'd forgotten the Continental custom of closing for a few hours during the heat of the day.

I attempted to sing about mad dogs and Englishmen going out in the midday sun.

"I wouldn't give up the library if I were you," Sam giggled.

"Shall we go for a look round now we're out?" I suggested, ignoring Sam's critique of my singing abilities.

"Might as well," Mark replied.

The apartment complex was close to a beach. However, it was more pebble than fine sand.

"What's that stone tower thing for?" Sam asked.

"Bonfires would be lit on it to warn of invasions and the like," I said, having read up about such things before we left. I chose not to admit how I'd learned this fact however. I was teased enough by the other two about my bookishness as it was.

"Was the island invaded much?" Sam asked, staring at the tower. I hoped he didn't want to climb it.

"Quite a few times," I admitted. "We, the British I mean, invaded. In fact Menorca was once governed by us."

"You seem to know a lot about it," Mark said.

"Uh…" I hesitated.

"He probably read a book about it," Sam giggled again.

"Yes, well." I ducked my head.

There was no one else around so Mark wrapped an arm around my waist and gave me a squeeze.

The three of us continued walking, but the heat was becoming oppressive, so we slowly made our way back to the resort.

As we reached the top floor of our block, the door opposite ours opened. The man who stepped out was huge. Not only was he broad, but I had to crane my neck upwards to take in his head. He had medium-length black hair and smiled broadly.

The giant extended a paw towards Mark, who was closest to him. "Hi, I'm Tom. I'm guessing you're English, otherwise you won't understand me and I'll be making a right prat out of myself."

Sam giggled, but did so from a position of relative safety behind me.

"I'm Mark, pleased to meet you." Mark shook the man's hand. "And, yes, we're English."

"Great!" The man's smile was huge…like the rest of him.

"We were a few places behind you at reception earlier."

I began to get worried. No way could I fend off a homophobic attack from this goliath.

"Mind you, you probably didn't notice us, you had other things to deal with." His smile grew wider still.

"Uh, yeah," Mark said.

Mark had the key, a pity because he was furthest from the door if we needed to make an escape. *Maybe the stairs would be a better escape route,* I thought, eyeing them.

Just then a man emerged from behind Tom. The new guy was pretty small—about the same height as Sam. The contrast between Tom and the guy behind him was startling, momentarily making me forget about possible exit strategies.

"Who are you talking to?" the smaller man asked.

Tom put one of his massive arms around the smaller man. "Love, this is Mark, and…"

"Hi," the smaller guy said. Then he chuckled. "We saw you in reception. Sorry, I'm Cliff by the way, and this big lug is my partner, Tom. You're lucky to get a double bed. We've only got twin beds, and you can imagine there isn't much room in one of those when your bed-mate is his size." Cliff pointed a thumb at Tom.

Tom held his free hand out towards Sam, who took it.

"I'm Sam, and the guy who's doing a goldfish impression is Simon."

My mind, which had been trying to get around the fact the two men in front of us were gay, too, finally realised my mouth was hanging open.

"Very pleased to meet you all." Tom laughed softly. "We were just about to go and get a few things from the shop. I'm dying for a cuppa."

I hadn't said anything up to this point, but managed to squeak out, "It's siesta. They're closed until four."

"I'd forgotten about that." Cliff slapped his thigh.

"Why don't you come in to our apartment?" Mark said. "We have tea bags, 'cause Sam here won't drink coffee."

"That's very neighbourly of you, thank you," Tom said.

Once we were all inside and settled on the sofa and some chairs from the dining table, Tom asked, "So, whereabouts are you from?" To Mark he said, "That's a Geordie accent if I'm not mistaken."

"I'm from Newcastle originally, but I've lived in Littleborough, near Leeds, for the past year or so."

"We're all from Littleborough," Sam put in.

"Ah, we're not too far away," Cliff said. "Tom and I live just outside York."

"Small world," I smiled.

"I know, what are the chances?" Cliff said.

"We've lived in or around York all our lives," Tom added. "We met each other at school."

"Simon and I bumped into each other in the street, became friends and then finally got together last Christmas," Mark said, sticking to the story we'd agreed some time ago. No one needed to know the exact details of Mark having to work the streets to survive.

"Like Tom said, we met at school." Cliff's eyes dropped and he began to pick at the hem of his shorts. "A group of kids were starting to bother me…"

Tom snorted. "It was a bit more than that."

"Yeah, well, and this new kid, huge he was," Cliff smiled up at Tom, "came to my rescue. And he's been my knight in shining armour ever since."

Tom blushed and shook his head. Looking over at us, he said, "Cliff's the real hero. You see, I'm not the brightest bulb on the shelf—"

It was Cliff's turn to shake his head.

"Me and him formed a double act at school. I looked after Cliff physically, and he looked after me mentally. He would help me with my homework every night. He would never do it for me, even when I begged him to. But he has a way of explaining things that even a thicko like me can understand."

"Tom!" Cliff warned. "You're not thick."

"Well anyway," Tom shrugged, "because of this wonderful man, I passed my O-levels, which meant I didn't have to get a totally dead-end job."

"What do you do?" Sam asked.

"Postman."

"Cool," Sam said.

I wondered if he was developing a bit of hero-worship for the big guy.

"And what do you do, Cliff?" I asked.

Tom answered for him. "I told him, with his gifts, he had to become a teacher. And a bloody good one he is, to. He has those kids eating out of his hand."

Cliff laughed. "You make them sound like wild animals in a zoo."

"Not a bad analogy," I smiled.

The conversation moved on to what Mark and I did for a living and what Sam was studying at school.

When Sam mentioned one of his favourite subjects was history, Tom chipped in and said, "That's what Cliff teaches." His face full of admiration he continued, "Cliff's head of department."

"There wasn't much competition for the post when it came up," Cliff admitted.

Tom shook his head at us.

"I want to study history at university," Sam put in.

This started a discussion on the merits of studying various periods in history.

I looked at my watch. "It's just gone four, so the supermarket should have reopened."

"My watch only says three," Tom said.

"That's because you're still on British time." Cliff smiled at him.

"Told you I wasn't all that bright." Tom took off his wristwatch and adjusted the time.

"Don't start that again." Cliff tapped Tom on the knee.

"Ouch!" Tom rubbed his knee.

"If those thugs in the playground only knew what a pussy-cat Tom is, they might not have been as afraid of him as they were," Cliff admitted.

We laughed.

I STARED AT the long row of bottled water on the supermarket's shelf, wondering which to get.

"The tap water here is taken from deep bore holes," Cliff told me. "You can drink it, but it's brackish…slightly salty."

"Really?" Sam said.

"So you're probably better off with this stuff." Cliff took a couple of large bottles from the shelf and put them in the basket Tom had insisted on carrying.

Mark spied a tube of KY, and put it in our basket. He had the sense to cover it with a packet of tissues, though not before Cliff had spotted what he'd found.

"Good, I didn't fancy having to go to a chemist's and ask for some," Cliff chuckled.

We returned to our apartment block and were about to enter our respective rooms when Tom asked, "Would you three like to go with us to the resort's main restaurant this evening?"

I looked at Mark, then said, "We'd love to."

"Shall we meet out here, say, half past seven?" Cliff suggested.

We agreed and entered our apartments.

As we were packing away the groceries, Mark said, "Tom and Cliff is a really nice couple."

"They seem totally devoted to each other. Did you see the way they look at each other?"

"It's just like you two look at each other," Sam observed from the couch, not lifting his head from his hand-held video game.

Mark took me in his arms. I managed to get the box of cornflakes safely on the worktop before they were crushed.

Sam groaned. "You didn't have to prove it!"

"Why did we bring him?" I nodded towards the couch.

"'Cause you love me."

Mark let go of me with one arm and we each used our free arms to beckon to Sam to join us in a group hug.

"Sorry," Sam soon said, breaking the hug, "I need the loo."

"Do you think you can flush it without help this time?" I asked his retreating form.

He turned round and blew me a raspberry.

A LITTLE LATER, Mark said, "We better start unpacking. Sam, you can have a cupboard in our room, and some hanging space in the wardrobe if you need it. I'm sorry you don't have your own bedroom, but they don't have many apartments with two bedrooms, and they would have been a lot dearer anyway."

"It's fine, thanks. I've just got a couple of nice shirts and a pair of trousers to hang up. Though I think I might wear one of the shirts tonight if we're going out."

"You'll be fine as you are. Save those things for more formal occasions," I told him.

We unpacked, had a quick wash, and it was time to meet Cliff and Tom.

There was no one on the landing when we emerged. Mark walked over and knocked on their door.

Cliff soon appeared. "Sorry. We were, um, busy…and lost track of the time." He blushed.

Mark laughed.

"God, those beds are small."

"Is your balcony overlooked by other buildings?" Sam asked.

"Sam!" I hissed.

"Erm, no, I don't think so, why?"

He giggled and went on, despite the glare I was sending his way. "You might think about spreading out the cushions from the sofa on your balcony, and…well…"

"Sam, that's enough," Mark said.

"I hadn't thought of that." Cliff went back inside his apartment.

"I hope they're not going to try it out now," Sam giggled.

I frowned. "That's enough, Sam!"

Tom came out then. "Thanks for the idea, little Sam. It just might work."

When Cliff emerged and locked the door, we descended the stairs, Sam and Tom in the lead. I was surprised at Sam's reaction to the big man; I'd have thought he would have been intimidated by Tom's size.

"How tall are you?" I heard Sam ask.

"Six feet seven and a half in my stocking feet."

"Wow!"

I lost the rest of the conversation because Cliff began talking to me. "He's a great kid."

"Yeah. We think the world of him."

"I take it he's…*family?*"

It took me a moment to work out what he meant. Nodding, I said, "He has a boyfriend back home. His dad's a builder, so they can't take him on holiday this time of year because they're too busy, so they let us take him."

"Do they know he's gay?"

I nodded. "They know about Mark and me, too. They're wonderful people. Mark and I think of Sam as the son we'll never have."

"I love kids. I guess that's why I became a teacher. But of course it's so hard not being able to bring one up ourselves. Tom would make a great dad."

I verbalised my surprise at how Sam had warmed to Tom.

Cliff smiled. "Tom's always been great with kids. They look on him as their protector. I should know, because he was mine, and I guess still is."

I thought about how much Mark protected me. Not necessarily in the physical sense, but on an emotional level. Where would I be now if it wasn't for him? I pushed the thought away, it was too horrible to contemplate, especially on holiday when I was having fun.

"Tell me," I said, "When you became head of department, did you miss having as much contact with the pupils?"

"Oh, yes, fewer classes and more paperwork."

"I can relate to that. I was a librarian…I met the public all day. Then I got promoted, and I hardly ever see the public anymore, and like you, there's a load more paperwork."

"I sometimes wonder if it was worth it. The extra money is nice, and I still get to teach, but the increased responsibility is a pain sometimes."

I nodded, thinking the same thing.

We'd arrived at the restaurant by this point. Tom held Cliff's chair out for him.

"He's such a gentleman," Cliff told me.

"I tried to do the same for Simon once," Mark said. "He told me not to be daft. Anyway, we don't feel all that comfortable about public displays of affection."

"I know what you mean," Cliff said. "As a teacher, I've got to be so careful."

"Can't be easy," I said.

"It isn't. I'm out to a few of my colleagues, and the head was great about it. I thought he at least needed to know in case of any trouble. You just have to make sure that you don't put yourself into a situation where you could be compromised. I mean, don't be in a room with just one pupil. Or if that can't be avoided, make sure the door is left open."

"Wouldn't that be true for all teachers?" Mark asked.

Cliff nodded. "Oh, yes."

"Hello chaps, hope you've settled in." Peter, the tour rep, approached. "And I hope you like your room." This was addressed to Mark and me.

"Yes, thank you," Mark said, with a note of finality in his

voice, basically telling the little shit that he better not continue with this line of conversation.

"Right then. Be seeing you all tomorrow at ten in the main lounge for our little getting to know you session."

"We'll be there," Tom said. His tone implied 'now push off'.

Peter took the thinly disguised hint and minced away.

We looked at the menus. Mark and I chose the paella. Sam stuck to the old faithful of teenage cuisine, burger and fries. Cliff ordered grilled sea bass, and Tom opted for a large steak.

"It's the only thing he ever orders," Cliff confided to us.

"I know what I like," Tom defended himself.

Cliff smiled at him.

The food, when it came, was plentiful and very tasty, though I balked at the shellfish in the paella, but it wasn't difficult to discard the bits I didn't care for.

We had a couple of bottles of white wine with the meal. Sam had a glass, but after he'd finished it, he asked for a Coke.

When we'd finished, a few of us began to yawn; it had been a long day.

"This one is so used to rising early for his postal round," Cliff yawned, "he'll be up at about four in the morning."

I saw Tom take Cliff's hand, but because of the table, couldn't see what happened next, though I could form an educated guess.

"I'm up now," Tom growled.

Cliff moved his chair away. Looking at Sam, then Tom, he said, "*Pas devant l'enfant!*"

Sam grinned. "*Je ne suis pas un enfant!*"

IT WAS RAINING quite heavily when we left the restaurant. Unlike English rain, it was pleasantly warm, but it was still wet so we didn't hang about.

"We'll no doubt see you in the main lounge tomorrow

morning for Peter's 'Getting to know you' session," Mark said when we'd reached our floor.

"Who does he think he is, Anna Leonowens?" Tom asked.

I smiled at his humour.

After bidding Tom and Cliff goodnight, we entered our apartment and Mark helped Sam make up his bed on the couch.

"Night-night, son."

"Goodnight, dad. Thanks for bringing me." Sam yawned.

"You're welcome. See you in the morning."

Mark came into our room. We were too tired to make love, and I wasn't all that thrilled about doing it with Sam so close by. We just held each other until sleep overcame us.

Chapter 12

A LOUD CLAP of thunder brought me out of a pleasant dream involving Mark, a large can of whipped cream, and a full suit of armour. I shot up and saw a flash of lightning through the French windows. The wind had also increased, hurling the rain against the glass. Maybe I should have closed the shutters before going to bed.

"Sounds a bit fierce out there," Mark said sleepily.

"I guess they know how to have thunder storms here." Usually storms didn't last too long in Britain. Rain, a few rumbles of thunder, the odd flash of lightning, more rain and it was all over in about ten minutes.

I got up and went into the lounge. There was a huddled mass under the blanket. "Sam?"

"Don't like it," a muffled voice said, almost drowned out by another tremendous crash from outside.

"It's all right." I patted the lump. "It's just a thunder storm." More flashes and claps of thunder followed, some making the windows rattle. The temperature remained quite warm.

"Budge up," I encouraged Sam. I thought it best to sit with him until the storm faded.

I ended up with a blanketed Sam lying along the sofa, his head in my lap as I stroked his hair. He soon fell asleep despite the continuing storm. I, however, took longer to doze off.

"SIMON, IT'S PAST nine!" Mark shook my shoulder.

"Huh?" I stretched and immediately realised I was sore from having slept most of the night in a seated position.

"We're going to be late for the meeting if we don't hurry," Mark said.

Sam stirred. "Thanks, Simon, for sitting with me."

He lifted his head from my lap and sat up. I stiffly got to my feet and stretched. "It's okay."

We ate a hurried breakfast, each visited the bathroom, and got to the lounge a few minutes after ten.

"Over here!" Tom hailed us.

I acknowledged them and approached the seating area they had reserved, stopping at the coffeepot on the way to pour two steaming mugs. Sam had orange juice.

"Pretty eventful night, eh?" Tom said as we took our seats opposite them.

"Why, what did you two get up to?" Mark fired back, keeping a straight face.

Tom had just taken a sip of coffee and began to cough violently.

Peter happened to be passing close by and approached. "Everything all right?"

Tom continued to cough.

"It's okay, I'm Heimlich trained," Peter told us, positioning himself behind Tom's bulk.

"No, no." Tom stood. "I'm all right," he wheezed. "Just went down the wrong way."

Peter nodded and went to talk to other guests.

Tom sat, cleared his throat, and took another sip of coffee. Looking at Mark, he said, "You daft bugger. I was talking about last night's thunderstorm."

"Yeah, I know." Mark smiled. "Sorry, I couldn't resist."

The rest of us were amused at Tom's situation and even he found it funny eventually. The coffee, I was glad to report, was good. I wished I hadn't bothered making a cup of instant at the apartment.

The five of us chatted until Peter started up his presentation. He was using a PA system. Although he didn't really need one given the medium-sized room.

He told us about some of the places of interest which we could explore ourselves or go on organised bus tours to visit, as well as a raft of other information about beaches, local restaurants and other touristy things. Patrick walked round handing out leaflets that went into even greater detail.

Peter said we'd have to book the bus tours fairly quickly as space was limited.

Mark, Sam and I decided to go on a tour of Menorca that concentrated on the history of the island. There was another tour that concentrated on the island's capital Mahón, which seemed interesting, too. The first trip left the next day, the second was on Wednesday. Cliff and Tom wanted to go on the historic tour, but seemed less interested in *Discovering the Capital.*

Peter then went on to talk about an evening visit to a Jazz club at San Clement on Tuesday night.

"That sounds interesting," Mark said.

I nodded. "But I doubt they'd let Sam in."

Patrick, who was passing, said, "Don't worry about that. He'll be fine." He gave us a smile and continued on his way.

Even though Peter had said space was limited on the various events, my canny nature suspected it was just a ploy to get us to book early. Nevertheless I handed over my credit card and booked the three excursions.

Peter then went on to extol the benefits of hiring a car. I felt increasingly uncomfortable. I'd only recently re-learnt the art of driving, and that was on the left side of the road. Having to drive on the right, combined with the stories I'd heard of mad foreign drivers, really put me off, but I was the only driver in our little family, so I guessed I'd have to swallow my misgivings and hire a car.

My unease must have shown because Cliff asked me what was wrong, and sheepishly I told him.

Tom smiled. "Cliff and I will be hiring a car. So why don't we get one together and I'll do all the driving? I'm guessing we'll want to go to the same kinds of places anyway."

"We couldn't impose," I protested, kicking myself for being such a baby about foreign driving.

"You wouldn't be." Cliff waved away my objections.

"But you two came away to be together," Mark said.

Tom shook his head. "Rubbish. It'll be great to have you three along."

"But you'd need to get a bigger car and…" I still wasn't comfortable with the idea of imposing on their good nature.

Tom laughed. "If you haven't noticed already I'm not exactly small. We have to get the biggest thing the hire company offers just so I can get inside it." Fixing me with a kind smile, he went on, "Unless you three would rather do your own thing. Sorry, I hadn't thought about that, I tend to take over and…"

"No," Mark interrupted. "We'd love to join you. We didn't want to impose."

"It's decided then," Cliff announced, folding his arms across his chest as if to end the discussion.

"We'll pay half of the cost," I insisted.

Tom said they were getting the car anyway, but Mark and I

stuck to our guns. Eventually we agreed that they would pay for the car while Mark and I bought whatever petrol we'd need. I still thought we were getting off lightly, but this was a holiday and I didn't want to make a fuss.

Peter announced the car hire rep would be in reception in a couple of hours, so we decided that once the presentation was over we'd go for a walk until then.

Peter eventually wound down. He knew his stuff, I had to give him that, but I wasn't convinced camping it up helped his performance.

"Believe me," Tom began once we were outside and heading for the path that ran along the edge of the beach, "I'm all for live and let live, but Peter is a bit much."

"I agree," Mark said. "Trouble is, the straights think we're all like him."

"Yeah, it's ridiculous. I suppose it's the fault of the media." I plucked a blade of long grass and began to run it through my fingers.

We started a discussion about the portrayal of homosexuality and other minorities on TV and in films. As the conversation progressed, I realised Tom and Cliff held similar views to Mark and me. I hoped, as they didn't live too far from us, we could become friends. We didn't have many friends at home, and none that were gay. It would be great to be able to socialise with another like-minded couple.

Looking at his watch, Tom suggested heading back.

"Do you drive?" Mark asked Cliff.

"Yes, but when we're together, Tom does all the driving. Like Simon, I'm not very confident behind the wheel."

Tom protested this, but Cliff merely shook his head.

"Simon started to teach me, but after a few lessons he told me he'd be happier if I got a driving instructor," Mark said.

I nodded, remembering the tense scenes in the middle of the empty supermarket car park after closing time.

Cliff laughed. "Tom taught me, though I think I tested his

patience at times."

"No you didn't," Tom insisted.

We soon arrived at the reception building. The blast of cold air from the air conditioning when we entered instantly chilled my skin, making me rub my arms.

As Tom waited to speak to the female car rep, the rest of us wandered around the large glass atrium, looking at the various display boards.

"Tom seems like an easy-going bloke," I said.

Cliff looked over at his partner and smiled. "People think because of his size he's a brute, but I've never met a kinder, gentler person in my life."

"When I saw him yesterday and he said he overheard me here at reception, I got an attack of the willies," I admitted.

Cliff laughed. "Please don't tell him that. He knows his size intimidates people. I think he tries to overcompensate by being so nice."

"I promise."

I'd been keeping an eye on the telephone booth next to the reception desk. When it became free, I reminded Sam he hadn't called his mum and dad. I should have insisted he do it the previous day, but what with being tired and meeting Tom and Cliff, we'd never got around to it. I hoped Paul and Helen wouldn't be too worried, although I remembered them saying they would understand if we couldn't telephone often. Trans-European phone calls were relatively expensive in the late 1980s. Few, if anyone, had mobile phones, so our only option back then was payphones.

After reading the instructions helpfully printed in English, German and French, not to mention Spanish, it seemed you made your call and the cost of it was printed out at reception, where you paid.

The instructions also gave details on international dialling codes, although me being me, I'd already researched them before leaving.

After pressing an alarmingly long sequence of digits, I listened for a few seconds while the connection was made. Once I heard the ringing tone, I handed the phone to Sam and left the booth.

He talked for a couple of minutes then beckoned me to the phone.

"Hello?" I said into the receiver, trying to remember not to shout. I don't know why, but I always felt it was necessary to raise my voice during long-distance phone calls.

"Hi, Simon," Paul said. "I won't stop on long, but I just wanted to thank you for looking after Sam last night. He said the storm was pretty bad."

"Yep, it did get a bit noisy, but Sam soon fell asleep when I sat with him."

Paul thanked me again and expressed sympathy for my uncomfortable sleeping position.

Mindful of the cost of the call, I said my goodbyes and handed the phone back to Sam for a final word.

By the time I'd paid for the call—which wasn't as expensive as I'd feared—Tom had finished with the hire car rep, so we went outside to the car park.

"Want to take her for a spin?" Tom asked, tossing the car keys into the air and catching them.

He'd hired a four-door saloon SEAT Malaga GLS in white. Mind you, most cars seemed to be white on the island.

Once Mark, Sam, and I were safely buckled into the backseat, Tom asked, "Where do we want to go?"

"What about Ciutadella?" Cliff suggested. "We could do a bit of sight-seeing, then maybe grab some lunch?"

"Fine by us," Mark told him.

Sam and I nodded our agreement.

As we neared the old city, Cliff said, "The Carthaginians called this place Jamma. It was the capital of Menorca until the British moved it to Mahón."

"He's off on his educated tourist routine," Tom laughed.

"Sorry. I forget sometimes I'm not in class."

"Please go on, it's really interesting," Mark said.

Sam and I agreed. Cliff seemed enthusiastic about his subject, which was more than could be said for the old crow who'd taught me history at school.

"I just picked up a few facts before we came. I thought it'd help me understand what I was looking at," he admitted.

"You sound just like Simon," Sam giggled. "He's always got his head in a book."

I shot Sam a look.

Tom chuckled. "But we wouldn't have them any other way."

Mark agreed.

Sam, no doubt in an effort to redeem himself, pointed out of the window. "What's that statue on the roundabout?" The statue in question was of a black stallion rearing on its hind legs.

"It's actually quite new," Cliff admitted. "It symbolises the *Fiesta de San Juan.* San Juan's the Patron Saint of the city."

Tom found a parking spot. We got out of the car and walked a short distance into a large square.

"What's this place called?" Sam asked.

The *Plaza de Born,*" Cliff told him. "That big obelisk over there is to commemorate the defense of the city in 1558 by the Moors. Now you see the town Hall over there, and the *Palace Torre Saura* opposite?"

We nodded.

"It should be open, but perhaps we could save it for another time."

I looked over to the harbour and saw the many open-sided restaurants I'd read about. My stomach rumbled. Because we'd slept late, we hadn't had much of a breakfast.

"We'll come back here to eat this evening if you three want to join us," Cliff said. "That is if you're not sick of the sight of us by then."

"Don't be silly," Mark told him. "We'd love to join you, wouldn't we?" he asked Sam and me.

I nodded. "It's a lot more interesting going around with a

group of friends." I hoped I wasn't too presumptuous in calling them friends.

Tom smiled. "Absolutely."

"It's settled then," Cliff said. "Shall we grab a sandwich? I couldn't help but hear someone's stomach rumbling." He winked at me.

Sam giggled.

"Then maybe we could do the tourist thing for a few hours before coming back here for dinner?" Cliff went on.

"Suits us," I answered, getting the nod from my family.

We walked up towards the palace, then down a narrow alley that took us into the oldest part of the city. I could feel the history of the place. The sights, sounds, and smells were all so Mediterranean. Cliff told us some of the buildings dated from the 14th century.

Mark wanted to get some traditional Menorcan sandals. I must admit they did look comfortable, and they were cheap, too. However, Mark balked at the idea that I would wear them with socks. Seems that was a big no-no for him.

I wore the sandals for a while but when they started to rub the skin across the tops of my feet, I reverted back to shoes and socks.

Before I knew it evening was drawing in and we were back at the harbour.

The restaurants had magnificent views of the sailboats bobbing in the water. Menus were posted outside each establishment, so we walked along and compared dishes—and prices.

We eventually settled on somewhere. I think Sam's choice was chiefly governed by the attractiveness of the waiter who smiled at us as we passed.

"The harbour isn't very big," I said once we were all seated.

Cliff nodded. "It's one of the smallest ports in the Med. I think that was the main reason why the Brits moved the capital to Mahón, because one of the largest natural harbours in the world is there."

Cliff said he would order a fish dish. I decided to follow his example. Sam thought he might try paella; he'd had some of mine the night before. However, you had to order it for two, so Mark agreed to have the same dish two nights running. Tom ordered steak…the biggest on the menu.

Cliff asked us what we wanted to drink. Tom declined alcohol as he was driving. Sam also turned down the offer of wine, so Tom and Sam had Diet Cokes, and Mark, Cliff and I decided we'd try Pomadas, which Cliff said was a popular cocktail on the island made from locally produced gin, mixed with lemon juice. It was surprisingly good.

I was impressed when Cliff ordered for us in Spanish. The waiter really warmed to us because of that.

When the drinks came, I asked Sam if he wanted to try a sip of mine. Judging by the expression on his face before he tried it, you'd have thought I'd suggested he take a swig of cyanide. However, once he'd sampled it, he decided he really liked it.

"Want me to order you one?" Cliff asked him.

Sam hesitated. "I've got this Coke now."

"I can take care of that." Tom moved the drink over to his place setting.

"Do you think the waiter would mind me having a real drink?" Sam asked.

Cliff shook his head. "They're pretty liberal about serving alcohol to minors over here, especially if they're having a meal."

"And you seem to have charmed the pants off that waiter, talking to him in his mother tongue," Tom put in.

"Castilian Spanish probably isn't his mother tongue."

"Oh?" I queried.

"Many of the islanders speak Menorquin. It's similar to Catalan which is spoken in the north east of Spain."

I was constantly amazed by Cliff's knowledge; no wonder his pupils thought so highly of him.

When Sam's drink arrived, Cliff proposed a toast. "To friendship. *Salud!*"

"*Salud!*" we repeated.

The meal was excellent. No doubt it was improved by our eating outdoors; watching the boats bobbing in the harbour, listening to the seagulls cry and feeling the gentle breeze waft across us. The congenial company didn't do anything to harm the experience either.

The topic of conversation turned to previous holidays, a subject Mark and I couldn't contribute much to, at least not about jointly taken holidays. Given Cliff's facility for language, I asked how many times they'd visited Spain.

"We went to Ibiza last year on the recommendation of a gay couple we know."

"But we hated it," Tom added.

"Why?" Mark asked him.

"Although there were some historical sites that were okay, the main focus of the holiday seemed to be on the nightlife. Our friends thought we'd like all the gay bars over there. But Cliff and I," he smiled over the table at his lover, "prefer something quieter."

"I'm glad we didn't go to Ibiza then," Mark concluded, echoing my sentiments exactly.

"Al and Keith think we're stick-in-the-mud's, that's probably why they suggested the place…to liven us up," Cliff said with a little bitterness.

"They're good friends, but they have an open relationship, and we don't," Tom added.

"What's an open relationship?" Sam asked.

Shit, I thought, how do we answer this one? Tom looked over at me, I shrugged and thought, you got us into this, so you can get us out of it.

"Well, Sam," Tom began. "Some gay couples like Cliff and me only sleep with each other. Our friends like to sleep with people other than their partner."

"You're just like Simon and Mark then," Sam declared.

Tom hid his smile behind his glass.

I realised Mark and I needed to have a talk with Sam about

not revealing personal information.

"Now then, little buddy," Tom addressed Sam in a masterly effort to change the subject, "what do you want for pudding?"

"I'm not sure if I've got room," he admitted. There had been a generous amount of paella served to him and Mark.

"Of course you've got room. Let's have a look at the menu."

We made our choices, though most of us selected something light. However, Tom and Sam decided they'd go for the chocolate gateau.

"I'll never get you slim if you keep ordering large sweets," Cliff admonished his partner.

"I'm a growing lad," Tom replied.

"Outward, not upward," Cliff smiled and shook his head.

Chapter 13

UNLIKE THE DAY before, the three of us awoke in plenty of time for breakfast. We'd talked Sam into trying it Continental style. Mind you, he had little choice because we didn't have any bacon, sausage, or mushrooms.

"Not bad," he admitted after chewing the corner of a croissant.

"They'd be even better if they'd been fresh," Mark complained.

He'd gone to the supermarket earlier in hopes of freshly baked goods, but the stuff on offer had been yesterday's as they hadn't yet received their delivery. The only saving grace as far as I was concerned was the lower price.

We showered, shaved, brushed our teeth and hair, and were on our way to the bus stop with a few minutes to spare. Tom and Cliff caught up with us about halfway there.

Morning greetings were exchanged, then Cliff asked, "Did you sleep any better last night than Saturday?"

I nodded. "Yes, thanks."

Sam grinned at me. The little shit knew what had been going on last night. I gave him one of my *don't you dare say anything* stares. Sam nodded and I began to breathe more easily.

The previous night, despite my reservations at Sam's proximity, Mark had been very persuasive, and we made quite a dent in the tube of KY that we'd recently purchased.

"As per Sam's good idea, Cliff and I decided to spread the cushions from the sofa on the balcony and, after laying the two twin mattresses on top, we enjoyed a night under the stars."

"Is it difficult to find beds that are long enough?" I asked Tom, steering the conversation onto ground more suitable for young and impressionable ears.

"Yes, we've got a super king size at home,"

"And it's next to impossible to buy sheets that will fit it. I eventually had to buy the raw cloth and make them myself."

"He's a nifty little seamstress when he gets going." Tom laughed at his partner.

Cliff exacted his revenge by giving Tom a light punch to his left arm.

"Ouch! That'll leave a bruise," he complained, rubbing the injured area.

"Big baby." Cliff smiled at him.

"Your big baby."

Although it was great to see a couple so in love, I grew a little uncomfortable at their public display of affection, especially as other people might be able to overhear. We were walking through an area that wasn't exactly deserted.

For once Sam's interjection was appropriate. "Give over with all this lovey-dovey stuff. You lot will be sitting with each other on the bus while I'll have to sit by myself."

"We can't have that," Tom announced, putting a massive arm around Sam's small frame. "I'll sit with you."

Sam beamed up at Tom. "Really? That'd be ace!"

Yup, I nodded to myself, there's some serious hero worship going on there.

"And who will Cliff sit with?" Mark asked.

"Don't worry about me." Cliff shook his head. "I'll be too busy looking out of the window and listening to the tour guide."

We arrived at the bus stop, and as there were other people present, we had to curb our conversation.

The bus arrived—over fifteen minutes late—but this was Spain and *mañana* was the most commonly heard explanation, usually followed up with a shrug.

We sat towards the rear of the bus, which thankfully was air-conditioned. Tom and Sam sat in front of Cliff, with Mark and me behind him. Even though Cliff said he would be fine on his own, I was determined to sit next to him for at least part of the trip. I well remembered coach tours I'd taken in the UK when I had to sit alone. I'd usually managed to immerse myself in the tour, but I'd never quite been able to forget that I was travelling without a companion.

The tour guide introduced himself as Alan and said there would be a couple more pickups before the tour would begin. A few more people did get on, though plenty of empty seats remained. I smiled to myself at having my suspicions about Peter's 'book early' tactics confirmed.

Alan began his spiel. "Menorca has been a staging point for different cultures owing to its strategic location in the heart of the western Mediterranean. This location has attracted, since the dawn of civilization, different peoples who have coveted the island as a stopover port and a shelter…"

He went on to describe what we would be seeing on the trip. I was getting really into it, and looking over at Mark, he seemed interested, too.

I loved how the Mediterranean sunlight caught Mark's fine hair. It was an effort not to reach over and run my fingers through those beautiful strands.

We got off the bus at various points of interest, being told to be back by a set time. I sat next to Cliff during part of the tour and engaged him in conversation when Alan wasn't speaking.

"He seems to know his stuff." I nodded to the front of the bus where Alan sat.

"He's making it interesting, too. It's a difficult balance to strike between just reading out a whole list of facts and making funny but less informative comments." Cliff paused. "This might sound a bit xenophobic, but I'm glad we're all English speakers here. I've been on tours with four different nationalities on the same bus." He smiled. "Imagine we're coming up to an interesting building, statue or whatever. The guide starts in the first language. 'Ladies and gentlemen, the object that will shortly appear on the right is an interesting example of…' Then in the second language 'the object we are now passing on the right is'…' Then the third speech begins 'the object we just passed on the right…' And finally for the poor buggers who speak the fourth language, they get 'The object we passed a few moments ago was…'"

I laughed.

Alan started up again. "I'm sure you haven't failed to notice all these strange stone T-shaped objects dotted around the island. They only appear here on Menorca. They're called *taulas*, which means table in Catalan, but no one knows for certain what they were for. Some people think they were a kind of roof support, others claim they were a religious symbol, and a third hypothesis is that they were some ancient scientific device like Stonehenge."

I had noticed previously that many of the *taulas* had U shaped walls around them. I asked Cliff if he knew what that was for.

He shrugged. "Like the *taulas* themselves, no one knows for certain."

❖

THE BUS TOOK us to the small fishing village of Fornells.

"Ladies and gentlemen," Alan began. "There's a very exclusive seafood restaurant here. Its lobster soup is delicious. Or so I'm told. I haven't tried it because it's over £40 a bowl. Once a year the Spanish royal family sails into the harbour and visit the restaurant. However, when they do, all the other diners are asked to remain in their seats whilst the royal family is sitting. It's considered impolite to stand whilst the monarch is seated. As compensation, everyone is offered free wine. However, what goes in must come out. So if you take full advantage of the generous offer, you might be crossing your legs until the King leaves."

I smiled, imagining the discomfort.

Although we stepped off the bus, we didn't venture into the restaurant. Alan's comments must have sparked something in Tom because he said he needed a pee. I thought he'd have to buy something in a café in order to use their facilities. However, just before I could suggest this, Sam spotted a Superloo.

Tom put in his money—complaining at the high price—and entered, none too easily given his large size.

As the door closed, Sam said, "Don't take too long, 'cause the door opens automatically after a few minutes."

"I know," came the muffled response.

Tom was able to conclude his business within the allotted time. When he emerged, Mark asked Tom to hold the door so he could use the toilet.

"No!" Sam said, standing in front of the door, barring Mark's way. Giggling, Sam continued, "It needs to wash itself. You'll be washed too if you go in."

"How come you know so much about Superloos?" I asked.

"There was a programme about them on the telly a couple of months ago."

We waited for the unit to cleanse itself and then Mark took his turn.

Cliff managed to take a few pictures of the beautiful and no doubt expensive yachts moored in the harbour. We'd bought a cheap point-and-shoot camera and Mark snapped a few pictures of Sam and me with the harbour in the background. Then Cliff got behind the lens and took a few of Mark, Sam and me. Sam wanted a photo of Tom, who was strangely reluctant, but Sam soon talked him round.

❖

THE BUS DROVE up a narrow, winding road to the summit of Mount Toro, Menorca's highest peak.

Stepping onto the tarmac, Sam asked Alan, "Which direction is Majorca?"

Alan pointed behind Sam, who turned around.

"Oh wow."

"You're lucky," Alan told him, "last week it was misty up here and we couldn't see much at all."

We approached the 16th century church which Alan had told us was tended by Franciscan nuns. On entering I had to remind Sam to take off his sunhat as a mark of respect. As we looked around the beautiful old building, they started playing a recording of César Franck's Panis Angelicus. I knew if I heard that song again it would remind me of the church on the hill.

Next we visited the gift shop, and I bought a few trinkets to take home. Sam got something for his mother, but nothing appealed to him to give to Paul.

"We've got the trip to the capital tomorrow," Mark reassured him. "I'm sure you'll find something there."

As the bus made its way back down the steep hill Alan announced, "We are fortunate in having José as our driver. He's driven down this narrow road many times. However, this is the first time he's done it in a bus."

His comment received the expected laughter from the passengers.

The bus then drove to one of the island's few large-scale hotels, where we had lunch. We paid a flat fee and could go back to the serving line as often as we liked. I think this was the highlight of the trip for Tom, and Sam wasn't shy about returning for seconds and even thirds either.

With about an hour still to go before we had to get back on the bus, the five of us went for a walk and eventually found a secluded spot where we could relax in the warm sunshine.

"It's amazing how much history is crammed into this little island," Mark said after a few minutes of silence.

"It's been described as an open air museum," Cliff responded.

Remembering some of the things I'd seen, I said, "The island seems to have had a fair few cultural influences."

"Menorca is, or rather was, strategically important," Cliff said, looking out to sea. "The Phoenicians, Romans, Vandals, Arabs, Spanish, British, and French have all left their influence here."

"I liked the gin which the English left the best," Sam put in.

"You would!" Mark made to cuff Sam's ear, but the teen managed to duck. "I don't think that was the kind of foreign influences your mum and dad thought you'd be exposed to while you were here."

"English gin isn't foreign," Sam countered.

We laughed.

"Well, yes and no," Cliff answered. "The gin on the island isn't quite like the stuff we drink at home. Although you're right, Richard Kane, the first English governor, though he was actually from Ulster, introduced gin-making to the island. You'll probably see it being made when you go on the trip to Mahón."

"Why aren't you and Tom coming with us on that trip?" Sam asked.

Cliff paused. "We thought you might want to spend some time by yourselves. We didn't want you to get sick of the sight of us."

"I couldn't do that," Sam said, looking up at Tom.

Tom smiled his biggest smile yet and patted Sam's back. "Thanks, little mate."

"Won't you come with us?" Sam asked again.

"Sam, Tom and Cliff probably want to have some time to themselves," Mark told him.

Tom looked over at Cliff; did his expression have a hint of pleading in it? Cliff gave a barely perceptible nod.

"It's up to Simon and Mark." Tom smiled down at Sam. "I'm sure they want to spend time with you alone."

Sam put his hands on his hips and, with a grin spreading on his face, announced, "They'll do what I tell them to."

"You cheeky little shit!" Mark yelled as he chased after a giggling Sam, who ran off down a footpath.

We could hear Mark remonstrating with the still fleeing teenager, though everyone knew it was only in fun.

Remembering our earlier conversation, I said, "About the trip to Mahón, Mark and I would love you both to come with us."

"Thanks," Cliff said.

Just then Mark came back with a wriggling Sam over his shoulder. Mark delivered a smack to Sam's upturned bottom before setting him back on his feet.

"Now behave," Mark said, smiling at him.

THE REST OF the afternoon sped by. We visited several more sites of interest. Personally I could have spent longer at most of them, but of course we had a schedule to keep. I hoped that one day we'd all be able to come back to the island and spend more time examining its fascinating past.

The bus dropped a tired but contented bunch back at the apartment complex.

"We should get the use out of the car while we've got it," Tom told us. "Do you want to go back to the old city and eat out again?"

Everyone agreed, so we separated to go to our respective apartments to rest, shower, and put on clean clothes.

❖

"ARE WE ALL set for the white knuckle ride?" Tom asked from the driver's seat once we were all belted in.

"Don't you dare!" Cliff said firmly.

"Don't worry, sweetness, I'll take it nice and slow, just like I did all through last night."

I dug Sam in the ribs to stop him from saying anything. From my rear seat position I could see the back of Cliff's neck go red.

"Just drive," was Cliff's only verbal response.

"We'll stop off at the big supermarket on the way back," Tom announced as we passed it.

"Thanks. We could do with a few things," I said.

I knew we needed more water. It wasn't until having to buy it in bottles that I realised just how much water we used in an average day.

"I'M SURE THE smell of the sea adds to the taste of the food," Mark said, taking a few deep breaths once we were seated at a table.

"At home we don't have the weather to eat outdoors as much as I'd like," Tom replied, picking up his menu and scanning its contents, no doubt trying to determine the size of the largest steak.

As he'd done the previous night, Sam sat next to Tom. Cliff was on Tom's other side. I was opposite Tom and Mark faced Cliff.

This restaurant was more crowded than the one we'd patronised the night before, so we had to be more careful about what we said.

Cliff decided to have a selection of shellfish in some kind of cream sauce. Mark chose the same. I wasn't overly hungry so opted for a green salad with fresh crabmeat.

Sam turned to Tom. "Like you, I don't like much foreign food. I wasn't even sure I'd like a continental breakfast, but I did. You ought to try the paella, the one I had last night was great, and they give you loads."

I glanced over at Cliff, who was looking at his partner. There was a long pause while Tom continued to read his menu. Eventually Tom closed his menu and gave a decisive nod.

"Okay, little mate, I'll have the paella with you."

Cliff's mouth fell open.

Noticing this, Tom asked, "What?"

Cliff shook his head as if he couldn't comprehend what had just happened. He got up from his chair, walked round the back of Tom and Sam, approaching Sam from the far side. Cliff held out his right hand.

"May I shake your hand? History has been made today."

Sam giggled and accepted Cliff's hand. Looking at Tom, Sam said, "I'm sure you're not that bad."

On his way back to his seat Cliff patted Tom on the shoulder. To Sam he said, "He is."

We decided to order the same drinks as the previous evening, much to Sam's delight. That boy was developing a taste for alcohol. I'd checked with Paul before we left, and he'd had no objections to Sam having the odd glass of wine with food. I hoped this agreement would still hold for the stronger beverage Sam was requesting.

The waiter approached. He was English. No doubt he was a student who had gotten himself a summer job to supplement his student grant. "Hello," he smiled. "Are you ready to order?"

We were and gave him our order.

The waiter left and a few minutes later returned with our drinks.

"I like these Pom…" Sam faltered.

"Pomadas," Cliff completed.

"Don't drink it too quickly, because you're only having the one," Mark told him.

Sam nodded and thankfully didn't argue.

I must admit, the food, when it arrived, was excellent. Even Tom seemed to enjoy his paella—if the way he cleaned his plate was any indication.

This time we all declined the waiter's offer of a sweet. We wended our way slowly back to the car park and piled back into the car.

"IT'S AMAZING HOW many British products they have here," Mark said, looking at a row of familiar breakfast cereals in the hypermarket.

"They have to cater to the tourists," Cliff told him.

As we stocked up on essentials, I was amazed at how cheap the alcohol was. I got a bottle of Menorcan Gin and some lemon juice. Sam spotted these purchases, of course.

"Only with meals," I told him before he could say anything. "And then just the one."

When our purchases had been run through the check out, I looked at the display on the till. *Bloody hell!* I thought, *they've made a mistake. I don't make that much in a year!* Then it dawned on me. The total was in pesetas. It was with some relief I handed over my credit card.

WHEN WE GOT back to the apartments, I agreed with Mark that we should decline any offers to spend the remainder of the evening with Tom and Cliff. Despite what they'd said earlier, they did need some time alone. We hadn't made any definite plans for the next day. I thought we'd just play it by ear.

So we parted on the landing and told each other we'd meet up around nine or ten the next morning.

It was still warm outside despite the onset of twilight. The three of us sat out on the balcony on the sun loungers. I managed to find the switch to turn on the balcony lights. They offered sufficient illumination to allow me to continue my Stephen King novel. Mark read a newspaper he'd picked up whilst shopping, and Sam amused himself listening to music on his personal stereo.

An hour must have passed before anyone spoke. Then Mark said, "This is the life."

I smiled, "Yeah, my angel, it certainly is."

"Do you want some cheese and crackers?" he asked.

I nodded.

Sam said he'd like some, too. "And can we open that wine you bought as well?"

I rolled my eyes. "Good idea, but you've had your limit for today."

"Why don't you have one of those cans of pop we bought," Mark suggested.

"Okay," Sam agreed, but I could tell he'd rather have had wine.

Sam went into the apartment to help Mark. They came back a few minutes later. Sam handed me the plate of crackers and slices of cheese. Mark gave me my drink and resumed his seat in the lounger next to me. I felt pampered.

I noticed Sam had a large bag of potato crisps.

"I'm hungry!" he grinned, helping himself to two of the crackers and a large slice of cheese.

A short while later I said, "It's a pity these loungers don't hold two people."

Mark smiled. "We can bring the sofa out here."

Sam rolled his eyes and put his headphones back on.

Ruffling Sam's hair, I got up and helped Mark lift the sofa out. Then I went back inside and turned off the balcony lights. We sat for a long while, cuddling in the almost total darkness, faint sounds of night insects and lapping waves floating in on the occasional breath of warm breeze.

"I'm the happiest man on earth," Mark said softly.
I gave him a kiss. "Nope, my angel, that'd be me."
Sam crunched on a crisp.

Chapter 14

BREAKFAST WAS BREAD rolls that I'd warmed in the oven. We'd eaten croissants the last couple of days so I thought we deserved a change.

Spreading marmalade on his roll, Mark said, "We've got that trip to the Jazz club this evening haven't we?"

I nodded, my mouth full.

"I don't think I've heard much jazz," Sam admitted, still chewing.

I swallowed. "It's not my favourite type of music, but if it's done well it's okay."

Sam shrugged, no doubt unconvinced. Like most teenagers he was reluctant to try anything new.

"As for the rest of the day, we'll wait and see what Tom

and Cliff want to do," Mark said. "After all they're the ones with the car."

Someone knocked at the door and I got up to answer it. Tom stood behind Cliff, Tom's arms wrapped around his smaller partner's shoulders.

"Come in," I smiled and stepped back.

"Sorry, are you still eating?" Tom asked.

"We've almost finished."

They entered, and I offered tea.

"It's okay, thanks, we've just had a cup," Tom said.

I stacked the plates and the cereal bowls in the sink; we'd deal with them later.

"Have you two booked the Mahón trip for tomorrow yet?" Sam asked.

They hadn't, so as we had nothing else to do, we set off for reception where I hoped we'd run into Peter. Glancing at my watch I saw it was almost coming to the end of one of the times he'd said he'd be available for guests. Maybe the *What's On* board might give us some ideas of what to do with the earlier part of the day.

"QUITE A DEPUTATION," Peter smiled at us.

"Hi." Tom was less ebullient. "We'd like to book a couple more seats on the trip to Mahón tomorrow."

Peter tapped a well-manicured finger to his lips. The other hand rested on his hip. "I'll have to see if there are any places left. You're very naughty for leaving it so late."

From my vantage point next to the revolving rack of postcards I imagined I could hear Tom grinding his teeth. Sam started to giggle, but I silenced him with a look.

Peter flipped through one of his ledgers, picked up the phone, and held a brief conversation in Spanish with the person at the other end. Hanging up, he announced, "You're in luck, gentlemen."

Peter wrote out the tickets, and Cliff paid him.

Sam had wandered over to Mark who was looking at the *What's On* board. Once Tom and Cliff had finished booking their seats, they joined Mark and Sam. Deciding it was too late to send out postcards since we'd be home before they'd arrive, I joined the others.

"See anything you like?" I asked Mark.

He turned from the board and treated me to a salacious smile. Then he licked his lips.

"On the board," I said, feeling my face get hot.

Sam giggled. I didn't bother trying to stop him; I was beginning to realise it was a battle I couldn't win.

A ride on a glass-bottomed boat out of Cala'n Bosc marina met with popular support, but we'd already missed the start of the morning tour and we felt we'd be cutting it too fine if we went on the afternoon tour.

I suggested a visit to a Naveta, a type of burial monument. The pictures looked fascinating, but the idea was voted down as being too depressing.

Tom floated the idea of visiting the military museum at Es Castell. Sam was up for that, but it found little support from anyone else. Besides, the town, if not the museum, was one of the stops on the Mahón trip.

Mark shook his head. "If we don't decide on something soon we'll have wasted the day."

Sam pointed to a poster for a water park. It was as good a suggestion as any. No one raised an objection, so that was our day organised.

"Are you sure?" I asked Tom and Cliff as we walked back to our apartment building. "The water park seemed as though it was mainly aimed at children and young people. Wouldn't you prefer to do something a little more…sedate?"

Tom smiled. "We're only five years older than you. That hardly puts us in our dotage."

"Sorry." I ducked my head.

"Those big slides looked like a lot of fun," Tom said, rubbing his hands.

We entered the apartment and dug out our swimwear. A couple of weeks earlier I'd been shopping and had bought Mark a skimpy and sexy white Speedo. He'd looked absolutely gorgeous in it when he'd tried it on. So much so we'd had an early night that night, although neither of us had gotten much sleep.

THE SCENERY AT the water park was fantastic. There were hunky lifeguards everywhere. Tom looked even more massive partially clothed. He drew quite a few admiring and shocked glances from many of the women present, and from a few men, too. I noticed Mark got a few looks as well; however, I comforted myself with the thought *look all you want, but he's going home with me.*

Sam had the best time out of all of us—especially when he persuaded Tom to lift him into the air and throw him into the pool. However, this drew the attention of one of the hunky lifeguards and who asked Tom to stop.

"We'll have to make a move soon if we want to be ready in time for the jazz club," Cliff told us when Sam and I had shot down the slide for the sixth or seventh time.

Sam groaned, but I was less bothered. Repeatedly climbing those steps was beginning to wind me.

We showered, then changed back into shorts and T-shirts before piling back into the car. This time Sam had gotten himself into the front passenger's seat.

"Thanks for taking us, Tom. It was fantastic!" Sam gushed.

"That's all right, little mate," Tom said as he mussed up Sam's hair. "I enjoyed it, too. I haven't done anything like that in ages."

WHEN WE GOT back to the apartment, I told Sam he should put on his long trousers and a dress shirt. He took the items from our wardrobe and went into the bathroom to change.

"It feels funny wearing long pants again," he said once he'd emerged.

"It's amazing how quickly you get used to wearing shorts," Mark admitted, looking edible in a tight pair of white cotton trousers.

We met Tom and Cliff at the bus stop. Surprisingly, the bus was on time, and within half an hour it dropped us off outside the club.

Although we had a good time—the music was good, the food reasonable in price and quantity—the jazz club was too smoky for us. None of our party smoked, so we felt the effects severely. I had to keep rubbing my eyes. I'd noticed over the past few days that many of the natives smoked; probably encouraged by the cheap price of tobacco products. Back home such things were heavily taxed.

We were tired by the time the bus dropped us off at our resort, so we bade each other goodnight, and promised to meet back at the bus stop the next morning.

"GOOD MORNING, LADIES and gentlemen. My name is Jenny, and I'll be your guide for this tour of Mahón, the capital of Menorca. We will also visit a few other attractions on the outskirts of the city." Jenny continued for a few more minutes as she gave a detailed itinerary. Our little group had adopted the same seating positions as on Monday's trip. I must admit my eyes began to glaze over as Jenny droned on. After the first stop—I can't remember what it was as it wasn't of much interest—I changed seats and sat next to Cliff.

In one of Jenny's few moments of silence, I nodded to the front of the bus. "Oh dear!"

Cliff chuckled. "She's fallen into the trap of trying to cram in as much information as possible into the shortest time. If people wanted all these facts, they'd have bought a guidebook."

I suspected most people had stopped listening; there was no way they could absorb everything she said, not without taking copious notes.

"I feel as though I should apologise as you weren't going to come on this trip."

"Don't be silly. Anyway, we've got about three hours of free time in the city, so we'll get away from the talking encyclopedia then."

I laughed, and Jenny started up again.

I thought the next stop would be of particular interest to Sam. It was a visit to the gin distillery. Inside the building it was possible to see—from a distance—the gin making process. I wasn't surprised we weren't able to get closer. Health and safety, as well as hygiene regulations, had to be observed. It was interesting to be able to taste the various products they produced. As well as gin, they made a wide variety of liqueurs. I allowed Sam to have a small taste from my sample glass, he didn't like the first liqueur, so he ended up only having a sip of gin with lemon juice.

Of course there was a gift shop. They sold the gin in various bottle designs; some were quite decorative but expensive. My gay aesthetics genes warred with my Yorkshire sense of thriftiness. After much agonizing, nurture won out over nature and we bought two plain green bottles.

"It'll taste the same, and you only spent half the money," Mark told me.

We went outside and met up with Tom and Cliff.

"What'd you buy?" Cliff asked, nodding at the plastic carrier bag Mark was holding.

I told him, as well as of my internal dilemma.

"You realise the gin is cheaper at the hypermarket."

I thought back to the bottle I'd bought there. "Damn!"

Sam giggled.

❖

THE BUS DROPPED us off in the centre of the city and Jenny told us the three hours of promised free time had begun.

I'd studied the booklets Patrick had handed out on the second day and wanted to attend the organ recital in the Church of *Santa Maria.* Cliff agreed he'd go with me. Mark, Tom, and Sam said they'd do some sight-seeing and we'd all meet up outside the town hall once the concert finished.

The sound of the organ with its three thousand-odd pipes was breathtaking. I'd hoped I'd hear Bach's *Toccata and Fugue*, but alas, I was disappointed; however, the music that was played was no less spectacular.

AFTER THE CONCERT Cliff and I met up with the others as agreed and walked round into the *Plaza de la Conquesta.*

A passing English tourist agreed to take our picture standing by the monument that had been erected in memory of King Alfonso III, who, according to the tourist brochure, conquered Minorca from the Moslems in 1287.

I couldn't resist a visit to the *Casa de Cultura*, which housed the public library.

"Typical." Sam rolled his eyes and followed me inside.

We spent the rest of our time in the capital looking round the shops.

My mother collected *Lladró* porcelain figurines so, seeing a shop that seemed to sell nothing but *Lladró,* we checked it out.

"Don't touch anything," I told Sam.

"Yes, Dad," he smirked.

Half an hour later and several thousand pesetas poorer we emerged, my aesthetics genes satisfied. I just hoped Mum didn't already have the three clown set I'd bought.

Sam found a bakery and bought half a kilo of *carquinyols*, a local form of biscotti. "They're for my dad. He likes almonds."

I was sure Sam wouldn't be able to resist eating them himself so I went into the shop and bought half a kilo for us to share. Hopefully that would satisfy Sam's sweet tooth.

The time grew near to rejoin the bus, so we headed back to the pick-up point. We were lucky on the last coach trip to have passengers who always managed to make it back on time. Unfortunately it wasn't the case on this tour. A man and woman, I assumed they were married, were missing when Jenny did a head-count. She said we would wait for ten minutes or so, just in case. In the meantime she said she would use the time to give us some more 'interesting' facts about Mahón.

I might have been willing to forgive the couple for being late if it wasn't for the torture that their delay put us through. They did eventually turn up. Apparently Mrs. Latecomer had gotten distracted in the *Lladró* shop.

THE NEXT STOP was a hotel where members of the tour could get lunch.

It was another fixed-price self-service, go back as many times as you want affair. Needless to say all five of us took advantage of this…some more than others.

Again we had a period of time after lunch to kill, so we sat out on the sun chairs which the hotel provided and dozed off while we digested our lunch.

THE NEXT ITEM on our itinerary was a trip round the harbour by boat. Unfortunately it wasn't glass-bottomed. However, it was nice to feel the salty breeze in our faces as the boat sped along. Perhaps it wasn't such a good idea to plan a journey over water just after lunch. There was only one person who showed any visible evidence of an upset stomach, and that was the lady who had stayed too long in the pottery shop earlier in the day. It was mean of me I know, but I didn't feel much sympathy for her plight.

The next stop was a visit to Es Castell. Among the battery of facts Jenny fired at us was that it's one of the most easterly towns in the Spanish territories and so is one of the first to receive the sun's rays in the morning.

As we walked around, it was easy to spot the military-inspired architecture. The central square used to be a parade ground.

Cliff told us the English called Es Castell Georgetown. "After King George III."

Wasn't he the one who went mad?" Sam asked.

"Well," Cliff paused. "That's still up for debate." He shook his head, obviously not wanting to get into a heavy historical discussion just then.

"Jenny forgot to tell us about George III," Tom said.

"I'll remind her if you want." Sam dodged, laughing, as Tom made to cuff him round the ear and four loud voices advised him it was in his best interests not to.

I HOPED TO take things easy on Thursday. We didn't have any trips planned, we didn't need any groceries, and all the gifts had been bought. Everyone else agreed to just get in the car and drive around the island.

We played a game of left or right. When we came to a road junction, someone would just call out the direction. Menorca's so small it's almost impossible to get lost…though we did our best to try.

The unspoilt views were breathtaking. It was a joy to come across small villages off the beaten track. We had to rely on Cliff's Spanish to get us through—although he admitted his linguistic skills didn't stretch much further than ordering food or asking where the nearest hospital was. We required the former, but fortunately not the latter.

By evening we all agreed it had been a very enjoyable day, probably one of the best of the holiday thus far.

Walking back from the car park, Cliff said, "I've got to get a suntan before we leave."

"Thought you didn't like sunbathing, it being unhealthy and all that?" Tom asked.

"If I come back without at least a slight tan, I'll never hear the end of it from the pupils in my form. 'I bet you spent all the time poking round old buildings and museums, Sir,'" Cliff said, mimicking a teenager's voice.

We laughed.

"You've left it a bit late to get brown," Mark told him.

"True. But I might get a bit pink. At least I can then claim I didn't spend quite the whole week in old buildings and museums."

AS WE WERE laying out our beach towels on the sun loungers Friday afternoon, Tom said, "At least we didn't have to put the towels on them this morning to reserve them, like you often have to do at some resorts."

"I know. The resort, the whole island, is just so laid back," Mark said.

"Can we go to the Karaoke tonight in the restaurant?" Sam piped up.

I groaned. The idea of listening to a group of half-drunk tourists trying to sing wasn't terribly high on my list of things I wanted to do.

"It's our last night," Sam persisted. "We might as well end the holiday on a high note."

"It's more likely to be a flat note," Tom chuckled.

Mark said, "Let's give it a try. If it turns out to be as bad as you say then we'll do something else."

This seemed to be a good compromise, so we settled back in our seats and soaked up the sun.

A little while later Sam got up, stretched, and said, "Anyone for the pool?"

Tom decided he'd join him for a while. This pleased Sam enormously.

"Better watch it, Cliff," Mark told him. "Sam's got a bit of a boyhood crush on Tom."

Cliff laughed. "He wouldn't be the first lad to take a shine to Tom."

It was too hot to maintain any serious conversation. I turned over to roast my back. Mark rubbed another application of suntan cream on me. I loved the feel of his hands on my back. Mind you, I loved them on any part of my body. I had to remain on my stomach when he'd finished.

"You can get up now, I've done," he said.

"Can't!"

"Oh?" He knew damned well why I couldn't move. He whispered in my ear. "Have I given you a hard on?"

"What did you expect?" I asked quietly.

"Can I feel it?"

"No!"

He knew I wouldn't let him as we were in full view of the pool and other sunbathers. Mark prolonged my predicament by continuing to whisper lewd comments to me.

I thought I'd exact my revenge however, and in a carefully executed sequence of moves, I leapt up, grabbed him and pushed us both into the pool. The cool water at least dealt with the problem I'd been having.

"You sod!" he said, spitting out a mouthful of water.

This started a game of catch, not that I tried hard to evade being caught. Sam and Tom joined in while Cliff watched on in amusement from poolside.

When we tired of larking about Mark and I got back on the sun loungers.

From the pool Tom held up his hands and asked Cliff, "Want me to do you?"

Of course Sam giggled.

"No thanks, I did myself," Cliff told him, turning a page in his book.

❖

"WELL," MARK YAWNED. "If we're going to this Karaoke, we ought to start stirring our stumps."

Looking up, I found the sun had gone behind one of the apartment blocks and my lounger was in the shade. I decided I was ready to go. I hoped I hadn't overdone the sunbathing and wouldn't regret it later.

We gathered our things together and went up to the apartment to shower and change. Mark had suggested we arrive early and snag one of the few booths at the back of the room. The booths were fairly secluded as they were surrounded on three sides by wooden trellising with creeping plants running up them.

Luck was on our side; about half the booths were empty when we entered. We settled in with soft drinks and a few pre-dinner snacks.

Peter began the proceedings by telling everyone this was a Karaoke with a Fifties, Sixties, and Seventies theme. "That doesn't mean you can all come up here and sing *My Way*."

A few people laughed.

"I hope you all have a good time tonight, because the emphasis is on fun."

Peter continued to work his audience, getting them into the spirit. As expected from a British crowd no one wanted to be first, so Peter sang a couple of lively numbers. I had to admit his voice wasn't at all bad. Although I could have done without him camping things up.

Eventually a few brave souls stepped up to the microphone and sang their party pieces.

We decided to stay, so ordered dinner and sat back to watch the entertainment. Some people could sing quite well; others were little short of terrible. One cute little girl, who couldn't have been more than six-years-old, sang *How Much is That Doggy in the Window?* She received enthusiastic applause when she finished.

Sam was the first of our group to go up. He delivered a decent rendition of *With A Little Help From My Friends*.

"Wow, mate," Tom said when Sam returned to the table.

Taking a big gulp of his Coke, Sam said, "I chose it 'cause if it wasn't for my friends I wouldn't have been able to come here." He gave Mark and me a big grin.

I put an arm around him and gave him a squeeze. "It was a pleasure, son."

Our meal arrived and we ate while a few others sang or made fools of themselves. The couple that had caused the delay on the Mahón trip got up and sang Sonny and Cher's *I Got You Babe*. I wished Mark and I could have gone on stage and sung that.

Mark must have picked up on my mood because he took my hand under the table and gave it a squeeze. "One day, love."

After we'd finished eating Cliff said he'd take his turn at the mic.

"If you sing Judy Garland's *Trolley Song* again, I'm leaving," Tom told him.

Cliff laughed and went up to look through the song catalogue.

"He didn't!" Mark asked.

"He did. It was in a gay club in Brighton. God, I nearly died. All the queens loved it though."

We laughed.

Cliff did a good job of his namesake's hit single *Congratulations*. He got a good round of applause for it, too.

When he returned to the table Cliff asked Tom, "Would I have embarrassed you in public?" He paused. "Anyway, they didn't have *the Trolley Song*." He ducked away from Tom's playful swipe.

A little later Tom got up to see if he could find anything to sing. I was getting nervous, I knew I'd have to go up sometime but wasn't looking forward to it. Tom took the microphone and sang *What A Wonderful World.* With his large frame, he was able to produce quite a deep voice. He was no Louis Armstrong, but he did really well nonetheless.

After Tom left the stage, a couple sang *Something Stupid.* I thought I might as well go and do something stupid myself, so walked over to the lists of song choices. They had *Moon River.* It wasn't the liveliest of numbers, but it was mainly on the level, so to speak, so it wouldn't tax my limited voice.

Mark gave me a hug when I got back to the table. "Well done! I'm proud of you."

A few more went up and sang. Time was getting on, and Mark hadn't sung yet. I told the others he had a wonderful voice. Mark tried to deny it, until Tom told him to prove that he didn't. Never one to duck a challenge, my man strolled up to the stage and began to look through the selections. He asked Peter something, who got out another list. Mark read this other list and then came back to our table. Surely there was something in that lot he could sing?

Crouching next to my chair, he whispered, "This song's just for you." He leaned forward and gave me a quick kiss on the lips. "I love you."

He left the table and went up on stage. The song's brief introduction ended and Mark began to sing.

Immediately the hairs on the back of my neck stood up, and a shiver ran down my spine. Mark was singing *Younger Than Springtime,* the most romantic song from our favourite movie, *South Pacific.*

"Oh, no," I whispered.

For many of the performers—including me—Peter had turned down the volume on the microphone allowing the music to somewhat hide their weak voices. But when he realised Mark could sing, Peter turned up the fader and allowed Mark's rich baritone vibrato to fill the room.

Momentarily tearing my eyes from the stage I saw that most people had stopped talking and eating and were looking at Mark.

"He's good," Tom said during the bridge.

"It's our song...the first film we watched together." I blinked and allowed the tears I'd been trying to stem to flow freely down my cheeks. That was my man up there. He was singing for me. My heart swelled with love and pride and...

Tom pushed a paper napkin into my hand. Mechanically I wiped my eyes and blew my nose. I didn't want to miss a second of Mark standing on that stage singing his love to me.

I was a total emotional wreck by the time the song ended; shaking from head to toe. Sam told me later Mark had received a standing ovation as he left the stage, a number of guests urging him to sing something else.

I was dimly aware of Tom talking to me as he led me out of the room through a set of double doors. We walked a short distance before he leaned me against the outside wall.

Patting my shoulder, he said, "It's okay, no one can see you, let it all out."

I nodded and continued to cry. "Our song. The first film Mark and I watched together."

He smiled. "I know. It's okay. Mark'll be out in a minute. Don't worry, me and Cliff will look after Sam. Go for a walk on the beach or something with Mark. You two need to be alone for a bit."

I nodded, accepting another napkin from Tom before he left. Mark came out a few seconds later, put his arms around me and gave me a hug. I was so out of it I didn't worry about anyone seeing us.

"Our song," I finally said when my tears had lessened.

"I love you so much," he replied, sounding almost as choked up as me.

Mark took my hand and led me along a path. We went down a few steps and walked along the gravelly beach almost to the water's edge. Then we walked for a while, hand-in-hand, not saying anything.

Eventually Mark stopped and turned me so I was facing the Mediterranean. I watched the moonlight being reflected off the waves as they gently rolled toward the shore.

"You okay?" Mark asked softly.

"It was from our film," I repeated, bringing on another round of tears, but they were short lived.

He smiled. "I had to choose something very special because you're very special to me."

This led to more tears.

Mark got down on one knee; I thought he was tying a loose shoelace, then I realised he was wearing slip-ons.

Mark pulled a small box from his rear trouser pocket. Flipping the box open the moonlight reflected from two matching gold rings.

Mark looked up at me. "I'd sort of prepared a speech, but I can't remember most of it now. Simon, I love you more than life itself. Will you marry me?"

I swallowed, my mind still in a fog. I'd been hit for six not once, but twice that evening. Despite that I managed to croak out, "Yes." I swallowed and in a stronger voice, repeated, "Yes, yes, oh God, Mark, YES!"

Mark slipped one of the rings on the fourth finger of my left hand and, after almost dropping it, I put the other on Mark's ring finger. He got to his feet and took me in his arms. We kissed and held onto each other, me shaking, hardly able to believe what had just happened.

I felt Mark turning me to face the beach. Sam, Tom and Cliff stood a few feet away, huge grins on their faces. They began to cheer loudly.

"You…you knew about all this?" I asked them.

"'Course we knew," Tom said, giving me a hug. "Who do you think helped him choose the rings?"

"But…when?" I asked in confusion.

"When you and Cliff were at that concert at that church in

Mahón," Sam told me. "It was really hard not saying anything the past couple of days."

I laughed. "Come here." I pulled Sam into a hug and kissed his cheek. "Thanks, son." I then gave hugs and kisses to Tom and Cliff, thanking them for their parts in the surprise.

"Oy! Stop it," Mark said. "You've only been married for five minutes and you're already going around kissing other men."

Everyone laughed.

I threw my arms around Mark and gave him an extra special hug and kiss. "You know, there's another song from *our* film that's appropriate."

Spinning him round and round there on the beach, I sang about how I was in love with a wonderful guy.

About the Author

HAVING READ ALL the decent free fiction on the net Drew could find, he set out to try his hand at writing something himself. Fed up reading about characters who were super-wealthy, impossibly handsome, and incredibly well-endowed, Drew determined to make his characters real and believable.

Drew lives a quiet life in the north of England with his cat. Someday he hopes to meet the kind of man he writes about.

CPSIA information can be obtained at www.ICGtesting.com
Printed in the USA
LVOW120106150113

315673LV00021B/432/P